SHADOWS OF NEMESIS

The Nemesis Series Book II

L.J. MARTIN

WOLFPACK
PUBLISHING
— EST 2013 —

Published in the United States by Wolfpack Publishing, Las Vegas

Wolfpack Publishing
6032 Wheat Penny Avenue
Las Vegas, NV 89122

wolfpackpublishing.com

Paperback ISBN 978-1-64119-358-0
eBook ISBN 978-1-64119-355-9

SHADOWS OF NEMESIS

Prologue

Nemesis, Nevada

I'm praying that in short order this will all be over.

I've left puddles of blood behind, some of it mine, but gallons of others. I've had a few hours to put it out of my mind, and enjoy the company of a beautiful woman. Maybe for the last time as my luck can't continue to hold out.

Even with a healing hole in my thigh and one in my side, I can't remember a time I've enjoyed more than Lizzy and me merely relaxing in her feather bed, sipping some fine New Orleans coffee she'd brewed.

Finally, just before noon, seemingly with some reluctance, she dressed and went over to the saloon and returned with a plate of food.

"Where's yours?" I asked, admiring the eggs, pork chops, and hotcakes.

"I didn't think it would be wise to let anyone over there think I had company, since half the world wants to put holes in your hide. You're my business and no one else's, at least for a little while longer."

And I don't think I ever enjoyed a meal more than partaking one while Lizzy Perlmutter watched me with eyes the color of a cornflower over a porcelain cup.

When I finished, she asked, "What am I going to do with you, Tag?"

"Doubt if I'll be around to be done with, Miss Lizzy, and am a little surprised I still am."

"You've seen the posters out on you?"

"I have."

"Tag, why don't you head west and we tie up in San Francisco, which I plan as my next stop, and where there's fifty thousand pilgrims to hide out among...until this all cools down. You'd look just fine in a beard for a while. Like I said, you could sit shotgun—"

"Still got work to do, Lizzy. You wouldn't want a man around who didn't do what he said he was going to do."

"If you made a promise to a ghost I guess you could break it. I knew your sister if only slightly, and she seemed one who'd want her brother to live, and live happy. It seems to me you've already done plenty to fulfill your pledge."

"Maybe, but I promised myself as well, and I promised Angel Sanchez. And besides, the sons-a-bitches killed the best damn horse ever to wear iron shoes and a dog that was a Hell of a philosopher and smarter by a long shot than his master."

She laughed, and I smiled.

"Well, I guess I wouldn't care for a man who wouldn't kill several fellows over the loss of a dog and a horse."

My smile faded. "And a sister and brother-in-law and two beautiful nieces."

"You do what you think you have to do, Tag Mc-Bain. I never knew a man worth his salt who didn't do just that, even if a woman hates the fact."

"I'm truly sorry, Lizzy, as there's nothing I'd like better than to head for the sunset with you. This is not something I like doing, it's something I have to do."

She sighed deeply, then offered, "I'm going in to see what's up in the place. If I learn anything about what's up in town, I'll come back out and let you know. Meanwhile, you should get a little sleep before things liven up this afternoon."

I had the hunch she knew I was there for Colonel Dillon himself, and maybe that I knew he met with Bridgid Fimple every Saturday afternoon at the Mystic Hotel, then she stopped at her doorway, turned, and confirmed it.

"You'll make sure Bridgid doesn't get hurt?"

"Damn sure, if it's in my power."

She paused before she continued, and her voice

got that same low quality that warmed my backbone. "And if you live, you'll head out to San Francisco?"

"Lizzy, that's an offer only a fool could turn down."

She nodded and left, closing the door softly behind.

My backbone continued to stiffen, and occasionally shudder, as I knew there was a fight coming. I could always tell I was getting near a battle when my mouth dried out and I didn't have enough spit to swallow.

Lizzy had a beautiful Seth Thomas clock in her drawing room, and if I looked at it once, I looked at it a hundred times as the afternoon wore on. I left the house only once and that was to grain and loosely saddle the gray. I'd given Jackson the mule to Angel and his brother along with a twenty-dollar gold piece, as it was the least I could do for the boys whose father had been killed on my account, and I wished them well with instructions to head out for the sheep county in south Arizona or into the San Joaquin Valley of California, where I'd heard there were huge herds, mostly tended by Mexicans.

I wanted to be upstairs in the Mystic when my target arrived, so I set out down the back alleys at 3:30. I was only seen by one woman, who was smacking a rug hung over her line. She paid me little heed.

There was an outside back stairway to the upper

floor of the Mystic. I took little time in mounting it and, happily, finding the rear upstairs door unlocked.

By the spacing of the doors, I could tell the front two rooms were the largest, and knowing what I did of Dillon, knew that he would select only the best. Both of them, to my surprise, were unlocked. So I flipped a coin, and entered the one on the left. Both had bay windows that stuck out over the boardwalk below, and the street could be seen for its total length. I presumed Dillon, even though he was having an assignation, a meeting he'd want few to know of, would enter by the front door.

The doors to the rooms were in slight indentations, and I'd opened the one I entered just a sliver, but because of the recession it occupied I could only see ten feet or so down the hallway. To my surprise, I heard footfalls coming down the hall. It was my plan to take it as it came. If my room was entered I'd confront them then and there; if not, I'd wait until they were in flagrante delicto, if my Latin didn't fail me, or in flaming offense, otherwise well occupied at the task at hand. There was something about finding holier-than-thou Dillon with his pants hanging on the butler's valet at the end of the bed that appealed to me.

With my eye to the crack, I saw Bridgid Fimple in her skinny bony best enter the room across the hall. It seemed I was in luck. I hurried back to the front windows and was not to be kept waiting long, as Colonel Mace Dillon came striding down the boardwalk right on time. The Hell of it was he had his nephew in tow. And both of them were heeled, each with side arms and the boy carrying a lever action.

That was good news and bad, as I had the nephew on my list as well. But I'd planned to make Dillon squirm for a good long time before I put one in his knee, one in the other knee, one in his personals, one in his gut, and finally one between his lying eyes—just to get him to quit screaming.

Then I wondered, was he bringing his young nephew along to give him a lesson in the fine art of pleasure-women? Or worse, for some other illicit purpose? Nothing would surprise me.

Maybe the nephew was some kind of a lookout and would wait downstairs, making sure no trouble came up the stairway.

Of course you couldn't see the rear stairway from downstairs, so I presumed he would accompany the Colonel up and perch himself on a bench at the end of the hallway, near enough to my door that one stride would put me on him.

Or maybe he would accompany the Colonel into the room with skinny Bridgid, or into the room I occupied. It could be that both of them would occupy separate rooms if they were to stay over until Sunday service. That brought a smile to me, thinking of them fresh from a visit with Bridgid, a very soiled dove, to a visit with Preacher McGregor to cleanse their souls until they could soil them again.

And I proved to be right, as it was a murmur of conversation and two sets of footfalls coming down the hall. I didn't risk keeping the door ajar, but heard the Colonel instruct, "Wait here. Don't be going down for coffee or a damn thing. You watch the door. I don't want to be disturbed. You know what to do if that damned Slade shows his face."

I smiled, him still thinking my name was Slade and not McBain.

"Yes, sir. I'll stay alert."

"Good."

Then I heard the door across the hall open and close.

I gave it fifteen minutes, by the mantel clock over the small fireplace in the fancy room I occupied.

Having no interest in alerting Colonel Dillon with gunfire, I flipped my Army Colt around and took a good grip on the barrel, opened the door, and stood so as to be out of sight of the bench and nephew, took a quick step out and caught him rising from the bench, looking as surprised as if a scorpion had been in his underwear and chomped down on his personals. The blow took him dead center in the forehead and he crumpled. I caught him and eased him to the floor.

I'll deal with him after my primary prize was taken care of.

I reversed the Colt, eased the hammer back and tried the door to give Dillon and Bridgid a bit of a surprise and found Dillon to be a prudent man. It was locked.

A boot to the door near the hardware took care of that problem with one hard blow from the heel. The problem then was trying to quickly recover from the pain that shot from wounded thigh up my backbone to the back of my neck, feeling as if I'd been the one whacked in the head with a heavy revolver.

But the anger coursing through my veins made me recover quickly and in two strides I was inside, to find Dillon scrambling—in the condition God had delivered him to earth—to grab for his sidearm, hanging on a doorknob to what I suspected was an adjoining room, and Bridgid sitting up in bed, the covers raised over her upper body as if she had something not seen by half the male population of Nemesis.

My best laid plans of a slow death were for naught, as he got a hand on his revolver and I had no choice but to let fly with a shot that took him in his prodigious gut and spun him back against the wall, knocking a nicely framed sampler flying. But he still had weapon in hand. I had to pause as Bridgid went flying by, screaming for her blessed mother.

Dillon, to his credit, got a shot off but it was way

wide. I shot him in the shoulder of the arm holding the weapon—again slamming him against the wall, and he dropped the revolver and couldn't make up his mind to reach with his remaining good arm to cover his still erect phallus, for the shoulder wound, or to try and stop the blood pumping from his gut.

"You dirty bastard," he managed, convincing me to slow down the process.

"You ordered your scum to burn my sister out, and she and her husband and her two beautiful daughters died over a trickle of water."

To my surprise, he looked guilty, and suddenly remorseful.

"I did no such thing. I ordered Cavanaugh to scare them off the place. To accept my offer to buy the place. The man reached for a weapon, and it got worse from there."

"That's a damn lie. Ignacio Sanchez saw it all. Cavanaugh shot him down in cold blood." He didn't respond to that, knowing that Cavanaugh would lie to him if the truth was better. So I continued. "Well, sir, you were, as the lawyers and judge would say, the proximate cause. And I'm the jury and executioner at the moment, the only one at hand."

"I'll pay you—"

Now, that made me angry, and I fell back on my old plan, and pulled one off, blowing apart a knee. He collapsed, and again my plan went awry as he fell within reach of his revolver, and reached for it, which encouraged my next shot. Rather than between his lying eyes as I'd planned, it took him behind his ear and put a goodly portion of his face across the wall behind.

He was no longer the well-dressed, well-groomed dandy. He was now a bloody pile of puss gut.

I took a deep breath and walked out to find the nephew, Seth Rheinhart, recovering and sitting up on his butt, his legs splayed out in front of him. His eyes were still rolling like a couple of buggy wheels. His rifle was more than an arm's length away and his sidearm still holstered.

"You were there when the Bar M was burned?" I accused.

He shook his head, trying to clear it, and I gave him a moment. To my surprise, he began to sob.

"I was…I tried to stop it. Cavanaugh was crazy wild. He offered to shoot me down if I got in the way."

"How old are you?" I asked.

"Seventeen, come my next birthd—in a month."

"Did you take part in killing my folks, my sister—"

"Your sister isn't dead," he said.

That took me mid-chest as if he'd shot me with his lever action.

I gasped, sucking wind for what seemed a long

time, trying to get that together in my head, then asked, "What are you talking about, boy?"

"Cavanaugh took her. Up in the mountains to a line shack where he would ride up a couple of times a week, taking supplies and such. She was burned, trying to fetch her daughters. The Indian had dragged her outside and held her down, to keep her from running back into the fire. Her hands were burned, but healed."

"Where is she now?" I demanded.

"Cavanaugh sold her."

"Sold her? You don't sell people."

"I only know what Cavanaugh told me. He was in his cups and bragged about getting two bundles of furs from a bunch of Paiutes or Shoshone for her. He used her until he was tired of her hating and cursing him, then he sold her."

"When was this?"

"A couple of months ago."

I couldn't help but wonder if the band I'd run across in the lava country might have had her prisoner. I might have been able to get her then and take her back to the Salmon country with me.

The nephew was still blubbering and I could make out him saying, "God forgive me, God forgive me," over and over.

I holstered my weapon, contemplating if I wanted to shoot down a sixteen-year-old whelp, to go along with the seven I'd already killed.

"Son," I said, my voice quiet so he quieted himself, "I can only hope you've learned something from all of this."

"I told the Sheriff, Wentworth, soon as Cavanaugh told me he had her captive—but he said I should mind my own business just like he was going to do."

"You told him?"

"I did. He made me promise that I would not tell my uncle or Cavanaugh that he knew anything about it, and I did—promise I mean."

"But Wentworth knew?"

"Yes, sir."

Then I heard noises from down below. Apparently Bridgid had put the town on me, not that I fault her for it.

I kicked the rifle into the room I'd occupied and instructed the kid, "Throw that sidearm into the room, back up to that bench and stay there. Your uncle is dead as yesterday, so don't bother going in. He's likely already making excuses to Beelzebub."

He two-fingered the sidearm out and threw it gingerly deep into the room, then backed up to lean against the bench.

I spun on my heel and ran to the head of the inside stairway coming up from below. Wentworth led the pack, huffing up the stairs, carrying the double barrel from my old City Marshal's office, fully cocked.

He was looking down, making sure he hit each stair.

"Wentworth!" I shouted, and he looked up in surprise, stopping midway up the staircase.

He made the mistake of swinging the muzzle up, and I shot him mid-chest. He yelled "Martha," as he flung his arms up and went over backward. But his wife couldn't help him. I could see it was the last of his wife's fried pullets he'd enjoy. Both barrels of the scattergun went off, blowing a considerable hole in the wall, and I could see nothing but the disappearing backs of his followers as Wentworth rolled ass end over teakettle down the stairs, and his cohorts scrambled for cover.

I hit the back stairway, and even with my thigh sending messages to my head bone to stop and rest before the leg gave out, I took the stairs three at a time.

In a galloping limp, I made the loafing shed behind Lizzy's house, sucked up the latigo on the gray, and pounded out of there at a dust raising gallop without a shot being fired behind.

It would be a long ride back to find my Paiute friend Knows-No-Horse and his people and, hopefully, my sister. But I could make that journey now, as my business in Nemesis was finished. I had her journal in my saddlebags and I expect she'd fancy its return.

I wondered as I pounded on, following the Trans-continental tracks west to find my back trail to the Salmon country, would my sister enjoy a move to San Francisco?

I knew I would, and to my great surprise, now thought it was one I might be able to make.

I'm glad I'm again McBain.

I rode out at a canter—a killer, a horse thief, a wanted man—and totally at peace with myself and what I'd accomplished.

Chapter One

Three healing months later....

It's been months since I took retribution on a half-dozen no-goods, and I now pray they rot in scorching Hell due to my administration of hot lead, a blade or two, and a bear trap. And I know them that disagree with a fella settling his own grudges are of a mind to stretch my neck—no matter the right of it. I know by the posters peppering the landscape.

It's damn nigh impossible to lay low when posters dot the landscape and when, no matter, you are driven to find kin who've been badly treated and have fallen on hard times. You can't question folks in order to find your baby sister, now three decades old, and stay out of sight of folks who might recognize your likeness.

Otherwise I'd be in the high lonely, where nothing but deer, elk, raptors, and the good Lord, would know my presence.

It's my third morning in the town of Stink, one of three mining towns on the headwaters of the Owyhee

River in southern Idaho Territory—and I've been here too long, resting up, licking my wounds.

The sister city of Reek and another called Commotion lie in a triangle with Stink, each about five miles from the other. The ones with smelly connotations to their names are so named due to the proximity of hot sulfur springs near enough to occasionally wrinkle the nose of inhabitants—but only on occasion when the wind doesn't favor. The towns weren't laid out due to their olfactory pleasure but rather due to silver and gold discoveries, mostly now played out. Tailings from hard rock mines and placer digs surround all three towns, some in humps as high as buildings.

I'm going to make the rounds of Stink one more time asking about my missing sister before I move on. So I tie up Rusty, my gray with unusual sorrel 'rust' spots on his chest, and Jackson, my mule, in front of the town's busiest saloon. I've found that one must ask more than one time to get honest answers, particularly when men are busy with other tasks, like gambling and swilling. When I get answers, it's oft times answers to questions I wish I didn't have to ask and answers I wish I hadn't received. I haven't been well greeted in this establishment but don't give a damn, and more particularly when admiring the cleft of a generous bosom.

It's answers I want, not comradery. It's answers I need no matter how it might redden my cheeks.

The smart alecky, plate-round-face, with the bulbous nose and ears a half-inch thick, is sitting shotgun on the far end of the bar, away from the bat-wing doors. He looks a mite ridiculous with a bowler hat perched too high on his fat, but thin haired, liver spotted noggin. As I approach, elbowing through drovers and miners, he's eying me like I'm something sticking to the bottom of his boot after he's crossed the corral, so I'm not surprised at his obnoxious greeting.

He wastes no time and curls a lip at me, then snarls, "Ain't this the third time—the third night in a row—you asked about that whore? The Hell of it is, saddle tramp, you don't look like you could buy a single goober if'n they was a buck a barrel, much less invest in a poke off'n one of our soiled doves." The fat man cuts his eyes away and spits a well-gnawed chunk of chaw into the spittoon near the base of his stool, then rearranges the scattergun across his fir-tree-trunk-size thighs with one hand while back-handing the dribble off his chin with the other.

After his insulting welcome, he smiles broadly, amused at his own attempt at humor. I clear my throat, quell the heat ascending my backbone to calm myself, then shake my head showing some slight disgust. Then to throw him off, I return the smile, only mine is tight as snake's lips. I lean near the man and get ready to say my piece and say in a low voice, barely legible over the roar and drunken laughter of miners and drovers and drummers who are engaged in or watching a half-dozen games of faro in the crowded, cigar-smoke-filled, saloon, "Friend, you don't know me and I don't know you. I admit I got enough trail dust on my hide to support a fair wheat crop, and likely I smell a mite like the south end of a north bound skunk." He guffaws, then when my tone hardens, stops, stares, and listens. "Now, that said, if you think I fear that cut off coach gun across a fat man's flabby thighs—a fat man with a fool's floppin' lips—I'll be happy to shove both barrels so far up your fat ass your tonsils'll get a couple of places to hide in the muzzles."

The fat man manages another laugh, but this one is far less enthusiastic. Then he again curls his upper lip and sputters, "You talk right tough for a man who ain't heeled."

Of course, he can't see the boot gun, a two-barrel .44 caliber, chafing my ankle. At the moment, it's itching to shatter his backbone if it could make it through his middle.

"Fact is," I say, tapping my right bicep with my left hand, "this one's a .44 and this one," I change hands and pat my left, "is a .45-.70, and I don't need much more." I know better than to get into face-to-face fisticuffs with a fat man of equal height and half-again or more my weight, as a man who minute-by-minute carries three hundred or more pounds is never weal—slow at times, but never weak. And a couple of inches or more—four or five or more in his case—of fat will absorb a mule's kick far better than my nearly suet-free body, after me being on the trail for hundreds of miles dining, when lucky, on skinny, bony, jackrabbits and rattlesnakes.

I'm currently rib-counting thin. On the run doesn't contribute to leisurely dining.

Now the fat man isn't smiling. In fact, he snarls. I'm close enough so when he tries to lean back far enough to swing the barrels to my gut, he goes off balance. When he does so, he's precarious on the stool.

With my right, I grab the barrels, wrench them up so they aim at the sky, and I shove the man, hard, with my left. Both barrels fire into the ceiling, as the fat man goes down, hard, on his back. Now shed of his coach gun. He hits in the corner like a flounder, flat on his back, with enough force to shudder the flimsy mining town saloon. Goober shells and dust fly, and he oofs loud enough it echoes in the instantly silent room.

With the place suddenly cadaver-quiet after the echoes of the scattergun blast, all eyes turned our way, dust motes drifting down, and gun smoke billows in the air. I brake the weapon and pluck out the two spent copper shells out and flip them over the bar. All this while the fat man tries to regain his breath. He rolls to his belly shifts his knees under him to get to his feet, and manages to rise with his legs under himself and arms extended like he's about to start a foot race.

I wait until he's high in that position, facing away, then place a boot on his hogshead barrel-size butt and shove. The fat saloon guard can't get his hands up in time, and his head crashes into the clapboard wall, knocking a hole and running his head clean through.

He's stuck.

And with both hands on the wall, his knees again on the ground, he's trying to free himself, all the time screaming like he's being dragged to a French guillotine.

Where it had been silent in the saloon, the place erupts in laughter. Apparently, the guard lacks popularity with the customers. None run to assist.

I can't help but smile and am grinning and bending to pull the fat man free, when I hear the swish of something. As I join the fat man on the floor, I catch a swimming glance of the bartender holding a bat.

Then all goes black.

Chapter Two

Nice jail.

A little nippy. But outside the bars keeping me inside is a little glazed window. Four expensive squares of real glass. It keeps the breeze out. And it seems I've been provided a decent blanket. The only heat in the room comes from afar. It's a pot-bellied stove I can see through the doorway in the proprietor's office—Sheriff or city marshal I presume—and. At the moment, I'm admiring it as it has a ten-cup blue porcelain coffee pot steaming atop its black cast-iron body. I smile as I recall the shotgun guard, with whom I had a slight disagreement, was even more shapely than the stove.

To say I have a small headache is like saying the Rockies are a small mountain range. The knot on the back of my head, a spot likely in need of a few loops of catgut as it's still weeping blood, feels at least the size of one of the Rockies' mid-size peaks.

Even though I didn't have time to wash my mouth with the Owyhee Palace's cheap whiskey before the fat man and I tangled, my mouth nonetheless tastes as if a flock of sage hens has been depositing their leavings there. I'd sure fancy a cup of the coffee I presume rests atop the pot belly. So....

"Anybody about in the office?" I call out but get no reply.

There are two cells and my neighbor mutters something from under his blanket atop his stone bunk.

"Pardon?" I say.

"I said, shut your pie hole. I'm still sleeping here."

"If you want to rest easy friend, why don't you wander over to the hotel and invest a half dollar in a room?"

"Very funny," the lump under the blanket says, then rises to a sitting position. "You get paid for being funny or just try and amuse yourself? 'Cause I ain't paying and you're the only one hereabouts thinks you're amusing."

The old boy has a full head of mostly gray hair, now pointing in every direction, a thin face and hatchet nose, a receding chin that makes the nose even more predominant, and, although as tall or more-so than myself, looks as if he might be able to slip between the cast iron bars of our cells. He puts his feet to the floor, pulls on his boots and walks over to the bars separating our cells.

"I'm Frank Feeney," he says, and sticks a hand

through.

I shake as I introduce myself. "Talbot," I lie. It's the name of a colonel I'd admired when I was under his command as a captain. "Nice to meet you. I served with a Feeney most of eight years ago. He lost his shakin' arm at Gettysburg. Any relation?"

"My people all came from the south—down Georgia way. And as far as I know, none made it as far north as Gettysburg." He pauses and eyes me carefully, then asks, "I don't have a flyer on you, do I, Mr. Talbot?"

"Flyer? You work hereabouts?"

"I do. Do I have a flyer on you?"

I laugh. "I ain't that famous," I lie, straight faced. Fact is I've ripped a half-dozen off trees along the trails in my travels. Thank God they're a bad likeness and have me thirty pounds heavier and with hair as dark as mine was when the war started. I came out laced with gray.

I stretch and yawn, trying to ignore the fact it seems like a smithy has taken hammer and tongs to the inside of my skull. "When does the real law show up?" I ask. "I'd sing a tune for a cup of mud, not that anyone would care to hear me sing."

He smiles and to my surprise, walks to his cell door and pulls it open. "You take it black or I got some fresh cream?"

"Bitter as a peach pit and black and hot as a foot

up a bull's butt is fine with me."

He disappears into the front office and comes back with a Sheriff's-model Colt strapped to his waist and a cup of coffee in each hand. His is fawn-colored crockery with a brown star painted thereon, and mine plain tin, but I don't complain.

After I burn my lip trying for a sip, I ask, "You a deputy?"

"Sheriff. I sleep in a cell on occasion. If you knew Mrs. Feeney you'd understand why."

Even with a throbbing head, that makes me smile. "So, how long am I a guest of your'n?"

"I wish I was having to hold you for trial for killing that rotten son-of-a-bitch, Higginbottom, but all you did was knock the wind out of him and cause the wall and roof to be holed. Fact is I hauled you over here to keep you from the clutches of that bunch of high-binders at the Owyhee. What started that?" Before I could answer he smiles and adds, "And, a'course, to be my excuse for having to spend the night watching my prisoner—the peace and quiet of my jail."

"Then maybe I should thank you for saving my hide?" I say with a crooked smile, then continue. "The puss-gut took umbrage at my asking about a lady I'm trying to locate, as I'd asked a couple of times already."

The Sheriff strolls back into the cell, plops down on the rock bench that serves for a bunk and asks,

"Maybe I can help. I pay pretty-close attention to what goes on in our little town and, as a matter of fact, in the whole Owyhee drainage all the way to the Snake. How would I know this lady?"

After searching the west half of Montana territory, the panhandle of Idaho territory, and now back to southern Idaho not far from where my quest began in Nemesis, Nevada, I'm still a bit embarrassed to describe my sister as being a soiled dove. But it is what it is and will be until I find her and give her the wherewithal to recover her dignity.

"A couple of years younger than myself, thirty, a fine-looking woman with red tinted hair who may have some trouble shown by the lines on her face as she lost two beautiful daughters and a husband in a heinous way. No fault of her own. It's my understanding she has sunk to working as a soiled dove, but her most distinctive feature are scarred hands. She tried to save her children from a ranch house fire and suffered for the effort."

"And what's your interest in this lady, Mr. Talbot?"

I lie again. "Seems her folks died back in Illinois and left her some property. Sizable property. I'm in the employ of an attorney there, tasked to find her and inform her of a farm and other things she now owns."

If I told the truth as to who I am, I'd be held by

this Sheriff until a federal marshal came to relieve him of the killer of six men, and to face a trial that would surely result in my neck being snapped by thirteen turns of a rough hemp rope.

He shakes his head. "Well, a lucky girl, particularly considering her current circumstance. What did you say her name was?"

He's asking, but he's looking as if he already knows about who I asked about. "Last I know she was using her married name of Macintosh, but she's used others. She headed down this way more than two months ago from Silver Valley."

"Sally Maddox, a pretty red-headed lass, was here for over two months. Never saw her without gloves. Headed out to Virginia City if what I heard was true. She worked the River's Edge Pleasure Den down near the Owyhee just out of town a quarter mile. You might learn more there. Suggest you don't go back to the Palace as they'll find some excuse to ventilate your hide, you show up there again. Your horse, the gray, at least I hope that's yours, or I stole someone's as he was the last one at the hitching rail when the Palace closed. Anyway, he's at the livery with that knot headed mule that was tied next to him. Som'bitch tried to kick me twice. Your stock, I hope?"

I nod, and he continues, "You'll owe a half dollar to bail the gray and your som'bitch mule out. I took five dollars out of your poke for the holes in the Palace wall and ceiling. Highway robbery but the highbinders agreed not to file a disturbing the peace against you if'n you paid up, so I took the liberty."

"It was worth it. If fact worth more to put that liver lip through the wall."

"Hell, I'd have paid two fifty to see it happen, but I was next door. By the way, when I got there they was waiting for you to come to so they could hang you from a rafter, arguing with some customers who sided with you and I settled it to your favor. So you owe me a tall wet one someday soon."

"You got it, Sheriff. When do I get out of here?"

"Anytime, so long as you promise to keep on going. By the way, don't let me forget your boot gun in my safe. Your Winchester and your LeMats are with your rig at Paddy McGuire's, the livery, along with your mule and packs. Looked like a coach gun in your pack. You come ready for a range war, sir." I don't respond so he continues. "Paddy's an honest man and what came to him you'll get back."

"Thank you," I say, sincerely.

"You sure I don't have paper on you, Mr. Talbot... or so you say. I seem to recall a poster about a fella with a pair of LeMats in saddle holsters—"

"Hell, Sheriff, there's lots of ol' boys came out of the war with LeMats. I'm in good company, and," I laugh, "I'd imagine some bad company, in that regards."

"I'd guess that's true," he says, and nods, seemingly satisfied.

He unlocks the door to my cell and swings it aside.

"I'm obliged for the coffee," I say, and shake again.

As I start out, the Sheriff stops me. "Mr. Talbot, I hope you're being honest with me in regards to Miss Maddox as she's a lady who's had more than a lifetime of trouble, or so I hear. She was in that fire, lost family, was a slave to a bunch of savages, then was traded to some lowlife Idaho pimp who in turn traded her to some bawdy house owner who in turn treated her badly. All this came to me second hand from…from a friend who works at the River's Edge who thought very highly of her. And the lady earned the respect of the whole town. I'd hate to hear you are not what you say you are."

"God's honest truth, Sheriff, I have nothing but best wishes for the lady."

He nods, and I leave. I'd been wondering how she escaped the savages, now it makes some sense.

I'm a little worried but after I'm out on the boardwalk, check my poke the Sheriff's dug out of his little safe along with my belly gun. I do it after I'm out on the boardwalk as I don't want to offend him by questioning my coin but see that I have nearly two hundred dollars in gold still intact. He's an honest man. I'm damn lucky he is and likely damn lucky he was within shouting distance when I got crosswise with the hooligans at the Palace.

The livery is between the jail and, on another quarter mile, the saloon and pleasure house next to the river. So, I stop and pay up.

Mr. McGuire is a stoic man, until I ask about the lady who'd worked the River's Edge, a woman who called herself Sally Maddox and who wore gloves upon all occasions.

Then he gushes her praise, and not about her skills in a horizontal position, as I have learned to fear hearing about. It's hard to listen with your backbone heating with anger—both at the teller and at yourself for allowing your sister to fall into such a gutter.

Mr. McGuire, I'm pleased to hear, gushes about her nursing skills. A talent I'd never been exposed to but I knew well her kindness and empathy for others which I would imagine are both prerequisites for being a fine nurse. It seems that the first week my sister arrived in Stink, a plague of yellow fever struck and she worked hard for nearly a month tending to folks.

I also learned why she left the smelly town.

It seems word came via the express company that she is among the wanted. It seems I'm not alone in that regard.

The son of a Silver Valley mine owner was found with a fish filet knife between his ribs, and a Miss Sally Macintosh wore a black eye, a split lip, and some bruises at the time and had been in the company of the son of General Theodore McTrippen just before the young man's body was discovered. Posters were going up across the northwest, advertising her worth, dead or alive, at $500. Hell, she's worth more than her older brother, whose dead or alive value is advertised at only $300, as it was only a cattle baron who received my wrath. Him and a few gun hands who got between him and me—gun hands who'd been responsible for the death of my brother-in-law and my two beautiful nieces and, I thought at the time, my sis.

Had we been valued by the body count, I'd be far ahead.

Only due to her good works saving a large number of folks from the yellow fever did the Sheriff allow her to move on. It seems his own wife was among those spared. Thank the good Lord he did look away from the wants of those Silver Valley folks, or I'd be headed back to Silver Valley to break her out of jail, if in time, or mourn over her grave, if not.

Her crime, by those who related it to Mr. McGuire, would be a self-defense, it seems, had the young man not been the heir of the richest mine owner in Idaho and her a lady of questionable morals.

It seems retribution runs in our family and I'm not ashamed of the fact, nor of her, if truth be known.

It won't make the finding of her, and her redemption, any easier, but it does make finding her even more insistent, if we're to keep ahead of the Silver Valley, Idaho and the Nemesis, Nevada law.

California is looking right attractive at the moment.

Chapter Three

I spend a short while at the River's Edge Pleasure Den as the chubby lady who is in charge there is very tight-lipped, and I think does not hesitate to lie to me about the intent of her former employee. Miss Maggie LaRue informs me that Sally Maddox lit out for Salt Lake City. She is a poor liar and only convinces me to search the opposite direction. So, I do.

Commotion is to the north of Stink. So, leading Jackson, Rusty and I head out that way, having to fork up a dime to cross the Owyhee on a ferry. The river is only a little over a hundred feet wide but running fast and deep.

I stop before entering the larger town and rearrange my gear. The Sheriff's comment about my variety of arms makes me a little nervous, so I untie my saddle holsters and hide the LeMats in saddlebags, and cover the coach gun so it isn't so obvious.

Commotion is a thousand or so feet higher than Stink and a more substantial town as two mines are still operating. Five saloons, a hotel with restaurant, another café, two liveries, a tonsorial parlor, a Chinese bath house and laundry, a substantial mercantile, an even more substantial bank—the Merchants and Miners—finely constructed of stone, make up most the main street, and a least four dozen clapboard and timber houses surround.

I see no sign saying Sheriff or city marshal, but a man with a copper badge on his waistcoat stands on the steps outside the mercantile with three others who look to be city merchants. I hitch my animals in front of the saloon next door, The Silver Dollar, but don't enter. As I head to the mercantile, the fella with the badge tips his hat at the others and heads my way. I pull my slouch hat low and touch the brim as he nears. He acts as if he is going to stop but I brush on past and push into the general store, going straight to a wall lined with tools. I buy a gold pan, a short-handled shovel and a pick, a pound of Arbuckle's coffee beans and a pound of salt, then head back to Jackson and add the tools to his load.

Now I look more like a man with placer mining aspirations than a man looking to engage in a range war.

Only then do I loosen the cinches on my animals so they can stand easy and push my way into the saloon to try my luck at finding my sis and to fill my belly as it has been a full twenty-four hours since I've done so.

A wheel of chance, four faro tables, and four poker tables all stand empty. Only two fancy dressed fellas adorn the bar. They look to be drummers, not law dogs, so I pay them little mind. Taking a seat at a table in a far corner from the batwing doors, I wait for service. I'm hoping a lady, willing to talk, will wait on me, but the bartender, looking a little irritated, rounds the end of the bar and saunters over.

"You think I need some exercise, or what?" he asks, only half smiling.

"Sorry, I figured you'd have a lady waiting tables or I'd have bellied up to the bar."

"Had a few at one time, but things have slowed down a mite. What can I get you?"

"Something to fill this hole in my gut."

"Got a fair-to-middlin' venison stew back there, with carrots, and turnips and spuds. Four dimes for a bowl half the size of your head and a chunk of bread bigger than your fist."

"Bring it on, and a beer if it's no more than the other dime to make up four bits."

He nods, then giving me a curious look, asks, "Ain't I seen you somewhere before?"

"Just rode in from Salt Lake, and Denver the month before. Headed to the diggin's in Coeur d' Alene. So, unless you spent some time wearing the blue I doubt it."

"I'll be damned. You sure look familiar."

I shrug. "Stew?"

"Sure enough." He spins on his heel and heads for the back.

The two fellas at the bar had turned to watch this exchange, then one of them, in a bowler hat and four-in-hand tie, rises and heads my way. Damn if he doesn't look familiar. I hope it's not someone who'll know me from Nemesis.

He walks right over and sticks out a hand, and I stand and shake, as he smiles and says, "You don't remember me, do you, Captain?"

"Captain? Did I serve with you?"

"Not exactly. You and your cavalry troop captured me and a dozen of my fellows at Pea Ridge. You were a fair man and treated us kindly, something I'll not forget. Can I stand you to three fingers of good bourbon?"

"If you'd oblige me with your name, I'd be proud to sit with you awhile. Invite your friend over."

"No need. Just met him at the bar. I'm selling farm implements and some mining equipment and he's peddling seed. I'm Alex Engstrom, formerly from North Carolina."

He fetches his drink from the bar, returns and takes a seat across from me while I eat.

My memories of the incident of his capture are returning. And I'm not eager for anyone to know my name, and not sure if he does.

When he settles in, he eyes me again. "I'm trying to remember your name, but it escapes me."

"Talbot. Hunter Talbot. Where did you end up, Mr. Engstrom?" I smile to myself at the given name 'Hunter.' As that was what I'm about these days, so it's as good as any and way better than most.

"Gratiot, in St. Louis. It was a Hell hole, but that wasn't your fault. From there I was moved to Rock Island, Illinois. I was paroled if I'd come west and been here ever since. How about you?"

"Here and there. I was never captured but took some shot in my hip and got retired and sent home, and as there was little home left, came west."

"So, is Commotion your home?"

"No, sir. Can't say I have a place I call home. I'm same as half the country, looking for the mother lode."

We talk until I figure I'd better make the rounds of the other places my sis, Sarah McBain Macintosh, might be or have been employed.

But, as had been the case for over three months, I come up with nothing but disappointment until the last of the saloons. Angel's Rest is anything but, and the black-haired pale-skinned lady with the bright red dress who seems to own the place looks to be more demon than angel, but when I ask about the soiled dove with the burned hands, she suddenly softens and pulls me over to the bar and signals for the bartender to bring me three fingers of rye. I start to complain but she says it's on the house, so I button my lip.

When I tell her the girl with the scarred hands is my sis, and I am hunting her to get her back in the family fold, I think she's going to cry.

She places a hand on my shoulder as she speaks. "She was going by Sally Maddox when she arrived, but all my girls work under an alias so I asked her to change. She was Sarah McKenzie while here and only here a little more than a week. She tied up with a big fella who called himself Will. Whole name he claimed was Wilber Dougle. She wanted to work her way back East. Said she might have folks in Cairo, Illinois, and he offered to take her up to Virginia City, saying she could go on north to Fort Benson and catch a packet or riverboat down the Missouri then another up the Mississippi to Cairo."

"Thank you, Miss…"

"Angel Angelo, formerly from Pueblo, Colorado. You be careful of this Dougle. It's my belief he's Wilson McDougle, who's wanted down Colorado and New Mexico way for a couple of train robberies and more than one bank. And in every case some innocents got shot down. Dougle is a huge man, wears a pair of converted Remingtons butt forward. He drew on a little fella here in my place. Didn't shoot him but damn near beat him to death with a revolver in each hand. He's got a real mean streak. I warned Sally—Sarah—or whatever her real name was, to fight shy of Dougle, but she was dead set to get on her way back to Illinois."

"I owe you, Miss Angelo. I won't forget."

"I thought lots of Sarah. She was pure of heart. You get her away from that lowlife if you can. He'll have her on that demon smoke, he gets the urge,"

"Opium?"

"You bet. He runs with a Celestial name of Hoy."

"Virginia City…what's the best way there?"

"Express coach if you've got the coin. Here to Bannack, then to Virginia City."

"How much is the fare?"

"Over a hundred dollars. Seems half the country is headed to a new strike up on the Madison. Every coach is loaded even at the exorbitant cost."

"How far, you guess?" I ask.

"You're two hundred miles plus change to Bannack—and you should search there as Dougle has cohorts thereabouts—then nearly another hundred to Virginia City. Hoy runs a gambling and dope den outside of Bannack aways. Good coach road all the way to both, so long as we don't get any early weather."

"And they went by coach?"

"Saw them off myself, ten days ago, begging Sarah not to go with every breath."

"Which of Commotion's liveries is honest in a trade?"

She laughs. "You ever met an honest horse trader?"

"Why I asked."

"Tomlinson has the best stock, if your buying."

"Trading. If I'm to get there before she heads out again, I've got to ride hard and can't do that pulling a mule."

"Tell Tomlinson I said to treat you right or he won't get a poke in Angel's ever again."

I laugh. "That should keep him honest. I'm in your debt."

"Get your sister the Hell away from Dougle. He'll use her badly and cast her aside, if she lives to be discarded."

I truly hated to part with Jackson but traded him for a sixteen-hand strawberry roan with strong black feet and the neck of a war horse. Even with the trade of a good mule it cost me fifty dollars in gold coin for the strong, proud-cut gelding and a saddle, rifle scabbard, and generous saddlebags. I cut my gear down to the minimum, stuffing coach gun into the roan's scabbard, the Winchester into Rusty's, and the LeMats and all my foodstuffs into the roan's saddlebags. I'll move the bags from horse to horse as I change as the roan's saddle would be a tad wide for Rusty. I split a half sack of grain between the bags.

It's heavy but as hard as I plan to work the horses, it's necessary. I knew the trail I planned to take, and grass would be a luxury over part of it. When I figured I'd distributed the gear as evenly as possible, with my weight, my Colt, and only the Winchester on the horse I would fork, I set out at a canter. It is my plan to ride ten or twelve miles, then change saddlebags and horses, so each animal would have a modicum of rest carrying only the gear which I figured at less than half my weight.

I start out on Rusty, dragging the roan, which I decided to call Roan, until he figures out it's easier to canter alongside and keep slack in the rope.

We leave out of Commotion in early afternoon and I figure at six o'clock, when it's getting too damn dark to see the trail, we've travelled twenty-five miles. If the stock holds up and they or I don't go lame on the rocky trail, we'll make eighty tomor-row—God willing and the trail not get too steep. The toughest of it will be dropping into and out of the Snake River canyon.

Then, just to spite me, it starts to rain.

Then, to add insult to injury, I overtake and swing wide of a band of what I figure to be Shoshoni, the Snake sub-tribe, or maybe Paiutes.

The Indians in the area have been peaceful of late, with the exception of the occasional missing horse or steer, but they eye me as I swing wide passing nearly a hundred feet west of them, and I didn't get a friendly wave—only a hungry look.

They are travelling north, as am I.

Then I realize they don't have a squaw among them. All braves. No paint. But I know that doesn't insure a peaceful bunch.

I ride hard into the night, until I hope I have two or three miles between us.

Now I must find a place to camp, in the dark, where I can keep my stock fed and water—and keep my hair.

Chapter Four

Seth Rheinhart, the nephew of recently passed cattle baron Colonel Mace Dillon, found himself the sole heir to over a hundred thousand acres of northern Nevada grassland. He had mixed emotions about his uncle and about the man, Taggart McBain, who'd shot Uncle Mace down in cold blood in his own study at the very desk where Seth now sat. Only in his twenties, the fortune sat well with the young man, but the stress and strain and constant pressure of a huge stock operation did not.

In fact, he hated it.

But it was his. And until he could find a buyer it needed to be maintained and protected.

He'd been pressured by some of the town folk of nearby Nemesis to do something to hurry the finding and hanging of the outlaw McBain, and he had mixed emotions about that as well. McBain had not only killed his uncle, but had methodically dispatched several more of his hands and the Sheriff of Nemesis. The Sheriff was a lowlife with a hand

out to Colonel Mace Dillon. So those in the know
didn't miss him nor blame McBain, but not nearly all
were in the know. For that reason, the Territory had
posted a $300 reward for McBain, dead or alive. But
that wasn't enough for some of the townsfolk or for
several of the ranch hands who had friends and, one,
a brother, among those McBain killed.

Seth was about to announce the increase of the
reward to an even two thousand—near to five years'
wages to men making a dollar a day and found—
which was the reason a gunman name of O'Bannon
had agreed to join the hunt.

The Hell of it was, Seth didn't blame McBain for
any of his misdeeds. Seth's uncle, in cahoots with the
Sheriff, had sent his men to run McBain's brother-in-
law, a small rancher named Macintosh, off his land.
The colonel wanted a spring flowing sweet water that
was on the Macintosh ranch, and water was dear in
northern Nevada. And the colonel's overenthusiastic
gang of ranch hand shootists, had killed Macintosh
in cold blood, burned the house, surprised too late to
discover two of McBain's nieces screaming inside.
Unknown even to the colonel, the sister of McBain
had been captured by the colonel's *segundo*, his
foreman, and taken to be used badly until she'd been
traded to a band of Indians for a couple of bales of
fur.

Seth had witnessed most of this and it sickened

him.

But still, he guessed he owed some satisfaction to the townsfolk and the ranch hands, and he now had plenty of money to gain same.

He walked to the window and watched the three men he expected to arrive this very day ride up the long lane to the ranch house.

Rollie O'Bannon was not personally known to Seth, but his reputation was. And the fact he'd hunt a man to Hell and back for a thousand dollars in gold coin, in addition to five hundred each for the Pollock brothers, was well known and even written about in Leslie's Weekly.

The three bounty hunters arrived as Paco, the Mexican houseboy and cook, was about to serve a round of chicken pot pies and a fresh baked apple pie.

Seth met the three rough-looking, trail-and-rail-car-worn men at the front door, shook with each and ushered them into the dining room.

"I got some decent brandy in the cupboard, if you'd care to partake?" Seth asked as they took a seat.

Arlo Pollock quickly nodded, followed by his brother, Jethro, but O'Bannon shook his head. "I do not partake of alcohol, thank you Mr. Rheinhart. It slows the reaction and there is more than one young-ster out there who'd like his likeness in Leslie's

Weekly for gunning me down."

"Leslie's Weekly?" Seth asked.

"You have not seen the write-ups on me? How then did you come to telegram me in Denver?"

"The federal marshal who came to investigate the Sheriff's killing mentioned your accomplishments."

"Humph," Rollie said, shrugging his very wide and thick shoulders. He was thick through—but muscle, not suet. "Your telegram said two thousand. Is that in addition to the $100 retainer you sent?"

"It is."

"We spent that getting here. So, I'll need another hundred for expenses, if we're to progress."

Seth sat back in his chair and eyed the six foot four inch two-hundred-fifty-pound bounty hunter, then said in a low but determined tone, "That's fine, go on or go home to Denver, but from now on any advances are against the two thousand, not in addition thereto."

Again, Rollie shrugged. "I guess we'll need to take this McBain, or Slade, or whatever his name is, down in short order, if that's the case. Any idea what rock he's hiding under?"

"Last word I had was that he was in Silver Valley, Idaho Territory, but he lit out from there headed for the Owyhee country in search of his sister or so it's been reported. Which is fine as it's much closer. He shouldn't be difficult to find as he's on prod to find the woman, not hiding under any rock. Turns out she's wanted as well, with five hundred on her head. So, you may get a bonus if you get the both of them."

"Let's eat," Rollie said, and the Pollock brothers both nodded.

"Paco," Seth yelled over his shoulder. "Serve."

Rollie, to Seth's surprise, removed his hat, bowed his head and silently said grace before he began, then ate like a gentleman, his cloth napkin in his lap, dabbing his lips occasionally. The Pollock brothers, on the other hand, left hats perched on heads, slopped their food, smacked their lips, gulped the fine brandy Seth had served, then yelled at Paco demanding a fill up. They cleaned their bowls and every crumb of bread on the table, stood, with an "obliged" coming from the biggest, Arlo, and both stomped out the front door.

"You got room in the bunkhouse for those two louts?" Rollie asked.

"I do," Seth replied.

"Fine, I'll sleep in the house, if that suits you."

"It's fine, so long as you're on the hunt tomorrow."

"We are. What's our first stop?"

"I'd say Stink."

"Stink?"

"That's the place. Seems there are sulfur springs nearby. It's the first town you'll come to in the

Owyhee drainage. It's a three-day ride. They have the wire in nearby Commotion and I'd like you to keep in touch. I'll reimburse you for the costs of communicating. If I hear anything you'll get word."

"If it's faster I could take the train back to Salt Lake and a stage north from there, while those two animals I work with take the stock?"

"I noticed they lacked civilities."

"That, sir, is a great understatement. They're as rough as a cob. I wouldn't put anything beyond them and am not too sure of their past. But they are tough as the hubs of Hell and show no mercy. If you're going to have a critter watching your back, it might as well be a grizzly—in this case two. Salt Lake?"

"By the time you wait for the train and hook up with a Concord for the trip north you won't save a whit."

"We'll have him in a fortnight, should he tarry. If you're not an early riser, we'll be gone with daylight. Now, if you'll show me to a room and ask that greaser of your'n to draw me a bath."

Seth couldn't help but smile at the man's audacity. But he nodded and rose to lead him upstairs.

"I'll take that hundred now, in case we're gone when you arise," Rollie said, and it wasn't an ask.

"Paco will bring it up with a copper tub. You can bathe in your room. How about the Pollocks?"

Rollie laughed. "Hell, they'd likely fall to pieces

you get the dirt and grime off that's holding them together."

Chapter Five

The lush grass country of the Owyhee drainage was giving way to the volcanic rock desert of the Snake, with its thousands of clefts and spires of black rock. I'd turned north off the east-west two-track the express wagon would follow a few miles back and followed an old Indian trail I'd come down on my first trip to Nemesis. The two-track wagon road had turned east to Idaho Falls, roughly following the river but high above, and crossed the Snake there via ferry, then farther north branched back west to Bannack City in Montana Territory. You could also turn east to Virginia City. The main road went on north to Helena and farther to Fort Benton.

I wanted to make sure I passed through Bannack City as Miss Angel mentioned that Dougle said he had friends there, even though he said Virginia City was his final destination.

It would mean we had to swim the Snake, but I'd done it before—if we got to the Snake with the band of savages seeming to take an interest in us.

The bad news is it's very rough going in a land of volcanic black rock that will cut the hocks and frogs of your animals, even though both mine were well shod. The good is it's damn hard to track on hard rock—even for a skilled savage.

I'm fortunate, the rain has stopped and it's clear with bright starlight.

As soon as I'm convinced I'm well ahead of the band I find a deep cleft with a necessary occasional wet spot, turn west, and we work our way at least two hundred yards off the main trail until I find a sandy bottom with some patches of dried grass and a trickle of water. It's thank fate for a halfmoon and enough light to see. I drop the saddles and bags, grain the horses, hobble the roan and, after I water him, stake Rusty, and find myself a fissure with a sandy bottom and spread my bedroll. With a supper of hardtack and jerky, I bed down. Won't do to have a fire as even if it or its smoke can't be seen from the trail, a savage with a good nose could smell it at this short distance from the trail.

I can only hope that they, too, found a place to rest for the night.

The coyotes, a night hawk, an owl, and the crickets sing me into a deep sleep, but Rusty's neighing wakes me, by the moon a couple of hours after I'd drifted off. As I worried I might have to come awake quickly I had left my boots on and rifle under the edge of my bedroll, so was on my feet with Winchester in hand in a heartbeat, then stood and listened.

As the roan is nowhere in sight, I figure Rusty is only jealous of his ability to wander with hobbles, so I work my way a hundred feet on up the cleft until I come on Roan working a patch of green grass beside a small pond and lead him back.

Rusty calms down as I stake the roan nearby.

Now, maybe I can get some rest.

I wake with a thin line of orange over the long flat rocky land to the west, flat and nigh treeless all the way to the Three Tetons, and we're back on the trail before the edge of the sun tops those magnificent mountains more than a hundred miles from our trail.

No sign of savages as we begin to drop the three hundred feet into the Snake River canyon. This is no trail to take lightly as it's pick carefully every step. As I'm yet to know the habits of Roan, I'm particularly careful. If he were to set back and lose his footing with the scamper of a chipmunk or flush of a grouse it could be the ruin of us all as there's a hundred-foot drop a foot to our right upon occasion.

But we make the river's edge.

And it's roiling higher and more angry than the last time I crossed. The sun is over the yardarm to the east so we have plenty of light. The last time I crossed the hundred-yard-wide river the horses were able to keep their footing for nearly halfway. But the river was lower, and I'm judging the current was some less.

I may have made an error not following the wagon road to Idaho Falls and the ferry, even though it would have cost me two days if I returned to Bannack City and more than a hundred and fifty miles.

But returning to the road would now cost me three days and I was likely to confront the band of savages again.

I took the time to give each animal a couple of palms full of grain as I knew, and should have anticipated even with good wrapping, the grain would likely swell and soon be worthless with the dunking into the Snake. I'd feed them all I dared as soon as we made the crossing—should we do so successfully. However, more and more as I eye the river, I question the fact we can make it.

But hesitation never accomplished much, so we plunge into the clear cold Snake, able to keep the horses' feet under them for a quarter of the width. Then I dump out of Rusty's saddle and let him tow me alongside, hanging on to the horn. With Roan dragging, the big gray has all he can do to fight current but he's up to the task.

We are near the far shore before the critters get feet to the bottom again, and the current has swept us a hundred yards downstream.

The bank is too steep to traverse, but I'm able to

lead the horses back upstream to the trail, occasionally in and out of shallow water.

We're wet, it's cold but not freezing, and we're in the shade of a deep side canyon for a half mile before we're back in sunlight. When we reach the flat again, I pause and take the time to feed the horses as much grain as I dare.

Able to see back down the canyon and across the river, I see a line of more than a dozen savages picking their way down the trail to the river's edge. I have an hour's head start and only ten miles or so before we're clear of the sharp volcanic rock. Then it's canter again and leave the Indians in the dust. I'll have miles on them before they can pick up the pace.

The next two nights are uneventful, with plenty of grass and enough water for the stock. After pulling up some low hills out of the Idaho flats I suspect I'm into Montana Territory. Then just before sundown I see the first sign of civilization since leaving Commotion—a fork in the trail and a rough carved sign. The left branch advertises the Big Hole; the right Bannack City and only a mile to reach there.

One establishment enjoys a location near the intersection of the trail and the wagon road to the Big Hole, Hoy's Tea House and Heavenly Pleasures, a long low clapboard building with three stovepipes poking through its shingled roof, and at least twenty cords of wood stacked up against the wall. There are no windows other than one of four panes in the door which is painted bright red to match a nearby carved Oriental dog as high as a man's waist. The hitching rail is long enough for twenty horses and already there's a buggy parked outside with a handsome pair of matched blacks and three horses spaced far enough apart you'd get the impression they didn't arrive together.

We can make it into Bannack City just after dark, so I ignore Hoy's and set a pace to do so.

The weather has blessed us; the Indians have stayed their distance; and a livery, rub down and warm stall awaits the animals.

All's well, so long as no one recognizes my ugly mug and someone knows something of the whereabouts of my sis. It's my hope this Dougle owlhoot has decided to spend some time in Bannack City and has yet to tire of my sister.

I elect to rub the horses down myself as the hostler wants two bits to do so, and I must be conservative with my remaining stash of gold coins. Besides, the three saloons in Bannack City will just be beginning to hum by the time I find a café and fill my flapping stomach.

As I head for a vertical sign as tall as a man advertising "GOOD EATS." I pass the post office and express company and pause to admire a half-dozen posters. I remove two, one of which proclaims that

Sally Maddox is wanted and one for Taggart Mc-Bain, my real name, and in smaller print, aka Taggart Slade. Hunter Talbot is not among the wanted, however it's a decent likeness of both Sarah and me. My compliments to the artist.

Wadded and chucked under the boardwalk, they'll be of little value—I   hope.

Now, after I stuff my gut, a sojourn into another damn saloon. I'm truly tired of having to admit my sister is a soiled dove and listen to tales of her dubious charms.

And of risking my neck being stretched.

Chapter Six

Rollie O'Bannon, erect in the saddle, one arm cocked with his fist at his side, after stopping to brush his clothes and comb his thick head of amber hair, rides into Stink as if he is in splendid uniform leading a Roman legion rather than a pair of hooligans who bathe only with a new moon, and then only if the temperature of air and water suits them. He makes enough of an impression that every horsebacker or stroller on the boardwalks, stop to stare and take in the sight.

He rides directly to Sheriff Frank Feeney's office, reins up and dismounts. As is their custom, Arlo Pollock announces, "We'll head to the whiskey trough to see what we can learn."

Rollie merely nods, mounts the two steps, pulls a neckerchief from his pocket, cleans the dust off his hand-tooled boots, and only then pushes his way into Feeney's office.

Feeney is leaning back in his oak chair, his feet up on the desk, snoozing.

O'Bannon stands a moment waiting for the Sheriff to awake, then moves back, opens and, this time, slams the door.

Feeney jumps and the wide-brimmed hat he has covering his eyes tumbles to the floor. He mumbles something and disappears as he bends to recover his lid, then quickly rises back up.

"Thinking about a crime and how to catch the culprit, Sheriff?" O'Bannon asks, then moves nearer and extends a wide hand.

"Something like that," Feeney says, and stands to shake with the big man.

"I'm Rollie O'Bannon, in your fair town in search of this fella." He spreads a poster out on the desk that he'd removed from a tree along the trail.

"Hummm... Taggart McBain, aka Taggart Slade. Don't believe I've seen Mr. McBain hereabouts. Three hundred dollars is a princely sum." He reads the small print. "I believe I've heard of this Colonel Mace Dillon he kilt. And another handful of fellas. He must be a mean sort."

"He won't be, when I catch up with him." O'Bannon doesn't mention the bounty has increased to two thousand. Why encourage competition?

"So, these posters aren't always too accurate. However it's been confirmed to me that McBain carries a Colt on his hip, a Winchester, at times a coach gun, and, a little more distinguishing, a pair of

LeMats in saddle holsters. Seen anyone heeled like that of late?"

"Fact is I did have a fella, called himself Talbot. Passed through here three or four days ago hunting a lady. But he was working for some attorney back in Illinois."

O'Bannon smiles tightly, then offers, "Or so he said. Which way was Mr. Talbot headed?"

"Had word the lady he hunted, Sarah Dougle, who ran with a Will Dougle, was off with her man to Virginia City, maybe with a stopover in Bannack City. I was obliged, being a lawman, to send notice of that to the Sheriff up in Silver Valley as that was the location of the dirty deed she was said to have done."

"Obliged, Sheriff. We'll be on our way after we grain our stock and fill our bellies."

"Suggest the café down the block, or River's Edge Pleasure Den, down by the river. Stay away from the Owyhee. They'll serve you burro and claim it's prime beef. You'll be headed the River's Edge way anyways. But the sun'll be down in a couple of hours. We got us a decent hotel."

"Obliged again, but I like to keep my boys on the trail. Wouldn't do to have them get soft. We'll stand you to supper, if you'd like to come along to this River's Edge?"

"No thanks. Got to get back to plottin' against the

owlhoots, and Mrs. Feeney will have a pullet in the pan soon."

O'Bannon shakes again, and heads out to run down the Pollock brothers, who are likely half-drunk already. The faster he gets them out of town, the better.

Civilization doesn't suit the Pollocks.

Chapter Seven

Good Eats is an understatement as Matia Etcheverry, his name is in small letters over the kitchen door, has given me no choice as to my supper. He walks out of the kitchen and says, "Welcome, what would you drink with your supper—besides vino, of course?" He speaks with a heavy accent.

I presume the menu is limited as a sign behind the counter says only, "Eat $.50."

"Coffee, after I eat, please," I say, and he smiles, nods and heads back to the kitchen. I know the food has to be good as the hitching rail outside is lined full with horses, and I have taken a seat at a short eight-stool counter—and it half full—as every seat at six tables is occupied.

Then he brings me soup, bread, a tomato-based spread for the bread, then a lamb stew with creamed corn and green beans on the side. A pewter pitcher of at least four glasses red wine comes with the meal. When I've cleaned the large bowl of stew, he returns carrying a pot and asks, "More?"

I have to chuckle, as I can't force down another bite. It's the best meal I've had since mama sent me off with the Union, so I decide to leave four bits plus a dime tip.

As I am sipping my coffee, a skinny little fella with one injured milky white eye takes the seat next to me and asks me that dreaded question, "Ain't we met before?"

I stick out my hand and lie, as I've been prone to do lately, "Hunter…Hunter Talbot. Don't believe we've had the pleasure."

"What brings you to Bannack City, Mr. Talbot?" he asks, as Matia brings him his soup without bothering to say anything other than "Good evening, Oscar."

"You didn't give me your name. Oscar, I'd guess?" I ask.

"Oscar Oliver Ogdon," he says, with a smile. "At your service, sir. I am the telegraph operator and run the assay office as well."

"That's a mouthful of 'O's if you don't mind me saying so."

"Not the first time it's been said," he says, with a smile.

"A busy man. I'm on a mission to find a lady who's been left an estate in Illinois. I'd be working for a gentleman in Cairo."

"Interesting. Must be a large estate to chase this

lady this far."

"Decent size, I guess. But even if small, a person is entitled to what's theirs. You might have met this lady. She has worked at several positions."

"Positions?"

"Well, the polite way of talking about a working woman."

"How would one recognize this lady…who frequents saloons, I'd guess?"

"You guess correctly. Her most distinct feature would be gloves, long gloves worn almost to the elbow. It's my understanding her hands were burned in…in an accident. So, besides the fact she's comely, she always wears gloves."

He stares at me for a moment, then suggests, "Try Holland's Parlor, three doors down. Lady named Sarah Dougle frequents Holland's with her husband, a big fella named Will Dougle. But she doesn't work, except to keep her husband company while he takes our money at poker. She does partake…and I don't mean demon rum."

I dig in my pocket for four bits and a dime tip and drop silver on the counter, then stand and offer my hand. "Thank you, Mr. Ogdon. I'm in your debt."

"Don't thank me quite yet. The lady partakes of the Celestial pleasures and barely speaks. Just stands near her husband, usually with hands on his shoulders as he never lets her out of his sight and touch, it seems."

"Where do they live?" I ask.

"Several rooms are upstairs over Holland's. Stairway from the outside in the alley and one inside as well. I've seen them heading up."

I drain my coffee, nod and hurry out. I leave my horses tied in front of Good Eats but dig into the saddlebags and stuff one of the LeMats into my belt at the small of my back under my coat and move with more than a little determination toward the well-lit saloon with a fancy gold-colored sign over the door. The rest of the place, what I can see in the growing darkness, is painted white with light blue trim, like some fine Dutch tableware I've seen which makes me believe that Holland is not the owner's name, but origin.

Flanking the doors are large-paned windows, panes a foot square and six high by six wide.

I stop at the window as two fellas push by me and enter, shoving the batwings so hard they bounce off the mullions.

The place is crowded with Faro tables, poker tables, with a pair of billiard tables, and a wheel of chance in the rear. The bar is at least twenty-five stools long, and full of men. Cigar and pipe smoke hangs low in the place. A fancy bronze spittoon is spaced every six feet under the bar and a towel hangs every three. Over the back-bar, a high-priced Brunswick of dark walnut matching the front bar, both likely hauled from the east, are mirrors, except for a six-foot-wide painting. A fine depiction it is, of a large-breasted woman, who's forgotten to be attired, reclined on a bear rug.

I see a big wide-shouldered fella, bigger than anyone at the table of six, with a fancy embroidered mostly purple waistcoat with arm garters matching the color, and a wide-brimmed white beaver hat, his back to the side wall. Behind him is an older version of the sister I remember from more than ten years ago, last seen as I boarded a Cairo train with a platoon of Illinois Union troops. She's easy to spot with white gloves to her elbows. She wears a peach-colored gown with substantial white lace. A lace hanky is stuffed in the bodice between where a man's eyes would likely drift. She stands with a hand on each of his shoulders, shoulders I presume being those of Will Dougle.

I adjust my own wide -brimmed soiled-and-sweated-through hat and push into the bar, elbowing my way between the drovers, miners and townsmen and move to lean on the wall behind Dougle with only a foot separating me from Sarah.

She glances over at me, her pupils wide, her movements slow, and nods without any sign of recognition. Then turns back to watch the game.

I am sporting a month's worth of whiskers, both

hair and whiskers laced with gray, not the coal black she'd remember. Still, I'm a bit disappointed not to have her throw her arms around me.

Dougle glances over his shoulder to give me a look that says, "watch yourself, trash." But turns back to his game.

"Sarah McBain Macintosh," I say in a low voice, but not low enough, as she swivels her head my way, moving as if swimming through molasses. She is knocked aside as Dougle's chair is flung backward with his rapid standing and spinning.

And he's reaching for the left butt-forward Remington he wears on his waist.

It seems this is not going to be a happy reunion.

Chapter Eight

Dougle is a half head taller than me and forty pounds heavier. So when I snake a hand out and grab his wrist before he can pull his Remington I've taken on a task. He grabs Sarah's arm with his right hand and pushes her away. It's his left he's reached over to his right side to cross draw, so I reach forward and grab that wrist with my left hand. He pushes Sarah aside then swings the right to club me away, but I duck it, and still holding onto his wrist come up on my toes and head butt him hard enough to gush blood from his nose.

He drops back a step as I'm drawing my Colt, and as his right hand clamps over his nose I club him with the heavy revolver. He reels a step back, is eyes swim a second, but he recovers, so at the risk of sending him to meet his maker—something I'm hesitant to do as I'm unsure of his relationship with my sis—I club him again, hard, up aside his big noggin, knocking his hat flying.

To my surprise, Sarah slaps me hard with one hand

then the other, moving quick for a woman smelling of opium smoke. I've turned loose of Dougle as he slinks to his knees, and grab Sarah with both hands. I do not want to call out her name for the whole saloon to hear, as she is a wanted woman.

But with her wrists, I shake her hard, and say three times, "Damn it, girl, it's Taggart. It's Taggart. Taggart!" But I might as well be talking to the wall.

Two of the other men who Dougle was playing poker with are on their feet.

And to my displeasure, one is fishing a badge out of his shirt pocket and pinning it on his vest.

I shove Sarah into the man, spin on my heel, and am lost among the crowded saloon patrons, ducking low and making for the front batwings. Now glad I'd left my stock in front of the Good Eats café, but if they are on my tail and inclined to use firearms I won't be able to unhitch, mount up and lead Roan before they can lay down on me. I go the other way. I never fancied being back shot.

As I turn into a four-foot space between the saloon and a tonsorial parlor next door, I hear a commotion as men crash out the doors behind me. I pick hooves up and put them down like a flushed whitetail deer— if I had a tail it would be flashing—and round the back of the saloon and head down an alley until I realize I am behind Good Eats. A fella down on his luck is standing at the back door and Mr. Etcheverry is handing him a tin cup which I judge to be soup as I edge past them into Good Eats kitchen.

Matia closes the door as I settle down. "You are in a bit of a hurry?" Matia asks, looking a little put upon.

"Yes, sir. To be truthful, I had a bit of a disagreement in the saloon. Mind if I cool my heels here for a minute or two."

"You left a generous tip. Help yourself to a cup of coffee while I tend to my customers."

I nod, and he pours me a cup then takes the pot and moves out into the restaurant proper. I don't know Mr. Etcheverry from Adam's off ox and can only hope he doesn't go straight out the front door to wave down the law dogs. But I can only hope.

So, I sip my coffee and relax. He returns and fills my cup again.

"Folks runnin' all over the street outside, Mister... Mister?" he asks.

"Talbot. Hunter Talbot." I stick out my hand and we make meeting official.

"Make you a deal, Mr. Talbot," he says, his voice taking on a shrewd tone.

"I'm always willing to deal, Mr. Etcheverry."

"See that pile of pots over near and in the sink?"

"I do."

"You scrub those to a shine and you can rest up in the storeroom, and I'll fix you a stack of flap jacks and a couple of hen eggs in the morning. Seems to me you should stay off the street."

I stick my hand out again, and shake. "You make a fine bargain, sir. But there's a favor I need."

"Sir?"

"A pair of quality horses are hitched just outside. A gray with sorrel spots on his chest and a strawberry roan." I hand him another fifty cents. "If you'd be so kind to take them down to the livery on the corner and tell the hostler to rub them down and grain them. Give him that coin and tell him he's got another half dollar coming when I come tomorrow to fetch them. Talbot, tell him if you would."

"Make damn sure those pots shine. And sweep the floor if you're a mind to."

"My pleasure."

In another hour, after the last customer has left, he locks up, locking me in I imagine.

I'm happy to discover a half-dozen fifty-pound sacks of beans, peas, and goober peanuts in the store room and lay them out to make a decent bed.

I'm wishing I could wander down and mount the stairs beside Holland's Saloon to its second-floor rooms where my sister is likely patching up Will Dougle. She seemed very attentive to the big lout and I hope I didn't kill him with the last hard whack I delivered—or they'll surely add another murder to my posters. She's had enough reason to hate me and delivering her from the life she's now leading will be lots harder, should she have cause to hate me even more.

This hasn't been exactly the way I hoped our re-union would evolve. Damn the flies.

We'll see if, on the morrow, I can work out a way to let her realize her brother has come on riding in on a proverbial white steed to rescue her. If she wants to be rescued. Of course, a body under the influence of the Celestial smoke doesn't always know they need rescuing.

Maybe I'll have to kidnap her, until she comes to her senses and her head is clear of the demon smoke.

Chapter Nine

"The Hell I am, I can't swim," Arlo Pollock rails at O'Bannon. They'd camped back on top the Idaho flat and been on the trail an hour dropping down to the river.

"I'll sink like a rock," his brother Jethro stammers almost in unison with his older and larger brother.

"Look, you two," Rollie says, trying to be patient, "all you gotta do is hang on to those broomtails you ride. They'll cross this like two seals in the ocean. I never knew you two to show yellow."

"Shove it, Rollie," Arlo snaps. "We ain't crossing this. Hell, it's as wide as the ocean and moving lots faster."

"When the Hell did you ever see an ocean," Rollie snaps back, obviously disgusted with his two cohorts.

"Don't matter. I ain't goin' ankle deep in that river."

Rollie sits for a moment, and calms down. Then, knowing he runs with two of the hardest heads west of the Mississippi, instructs, "Go back to the wagon road, east two days to Idaho Falls, north a day or more to a cutoff to Bannack City, and I'll meet you there. I'm telling you right now, I have McBain in a cell when you get there and I'm keeping the whole gol'damn bounty. You got it?"

"To Hell with the bounty. We can't spend our share in Hell."

"If he's not in Bannack City, I'll be riding that same wagon road on my way to Virginia City— should the scum lead another way, I'll leave word with the local law. You got it?"

"We got it, we got it. See you on the trail or in Bannack City."

With that the spun their horses and started back up out of the canyon.

***

I awake rested, even if a bed of goober peanuts, beans, and peas is a mite rough. I'd snuggled in, blanketed myself with soiled tablecloths, and made myself a decent nest.

I had the stove stoked up and a pot of coffee on when, just before sun up, Matia unlocks his front door and strides through to the back.

He pours himself a cup and gives me a nod. "You get straight with the law and I can use a swamper. Those pots look fine."

I flash him a smile. "Your coffee is a damn sight better than mine. I fear you'd give me the boot before a day was through."

"Likely," he says, but laughs, then adds, "it seems a fella was beat down with a Colt, last night in Hollands, much like that one on your hip."

"No surprise to me or my Colt. Is he alive?"

"He is, and recovering in a room over Holland's accompanied by his wife, after a trip to Doc Henderson for some needle work. That Dougle is big as a draft horse. You had to put something behind that Colt to drop him."

"The bigger they are, the harder they put their face in the goober shells." I give him a shrug and a smile, then add, "Well, sir, I pray she's not his wife, only accompanying him."

"That would hardly be proper," Matia says.

"What goes on in a bawdy house that's proper?"

"Suppose that's right. Is that what this is all about. You have a hankering for his woman?"

"You have proven to be a trustworthy soul, so I'll fess up you promise to keep it under your hat." He nods, and I enforce the request, "My life could depend on your discretion." He hesitates, but then nods again. "She's my sister and he's got her in a bad way with that poppy sap some fools smoke. I plan to get her away and well."

He eyes me for a moment, then nods. "I'd guess

that an admirable ambition. Is she wanting to be tak-
en away?"

"To be truthful, I don't give a damn. I'll ask her
that question after I know she's in her right mind."

"Can't argue with your reasoning. Let's talk while
I whip us up some breakfast. I'm open in twenty
minutes."

***

Will Dougle was prone on the bed, holding his head
with one hand. Both his eyes were blackened and his
nose swollen. He was not a particularly handsome
man to begin with and now looked downright fearful.

Sarah was up and dressed only in her stockings,
pantaloons, and a light cotton blouse over a corset
that she needed only to give lift to generous breasts.
She poured water from a white porcelain pitcher into
a bowl on the chest of drawers to wash her face, but
first filled a cup and took it to Dougle's bedside.

"Will, why don't you get some water down. We
got to go out to Hoy's today. I filled my pipe with the
last of it this morning."

"I ain't going nowhere until this herd of horses
stops galloping around in my head. Who the Hell
was that no account son of a bitch that took a shine
to you?"

"What.... I don't remember anyone—"

"Damn, woman, you got to lay off that pipe or you won't be worth spit. If you think I'm going to Hoy's, you're pissing in the wind."

"I gotta go."

"Later. That fella you don't remember called you Sarah McBain Macintosh. I never knowed the Mc-Bain part, but wasn't Macintosh the name you left behind in Silver Valley?"

"It was. And McBain was my family name before I married."

"So, who the Hell was the saddle tramp who recognized you?"

"Will, I don't know. I barely remember going to Doc Hendersons with you. Want this water?"

Dougle rolled to his side and kicked her, hard, in the thigh. The coffee cup she'd used for water flew and broke and she spun away and sunk to her knees, then lay on the floor and began to sob.

"Damn," Dougle growled, "if you ain't gettin' to be a worthless pile of horse crap. I swear—"

"I'm sorry, I'm sorry," she sobbed, then quieted. After laying there for a few moments, asked, "I'll need a dollar—"

"Go to Hell. Hoy owes me. You walk out there if you gotta have some smoke. I ain't moving until this head stops pounding. Then I'm going on the hunt for that saddle tramp who clubbed me from behind."

He knew that wasn't exactly the way it happened,

but he wasn't about to admit he'd been head-butted by a man a half head shorter than he was, had his gun hand trapped, then been bludgeoned to the floor.

"Now," he said, "shut the Hell up while I get some more shuteye."

"I'll be real quiet," she said, and rubbed her thigh and whimpered, but silently.

When she was sure he was asleep and snoring soundly, she went to the bedside stand, opened the drawer, and took a five-dollar gold piece from his stash. Then she moved to the chest of drawers, re-turned, and quietly pulled on an ankle-length skirt, a bonnet, and a jacket. Taking her button shoes and the hook, and her reticule, she moved quietly to the door and out, silently, to the stairway. She sat and buttoned up her ankle highs, then headed out for the mile walk out to Hoys. She was in a sweat after only a block and it was cold out. The sweat had to come from the lack of what she sought, so she hurried.

Matia Etcheverry was pouring a customer a cup of coffee when he saw the Dougle woman pass, seem-ingly in a hurry.

He warmed up three other customer's coffee cups, then headed to the back.

I am washing up a few breakfast dishes, doing a little more than I'd agreed to, when Matia strides into the kitchen and up to me. "That woman?"

"My sister?"

"I guess so. She just walked by and seemed in a hurry."

"And Dougle?"

"She was alone."

I stick out my hand and shake with Matia. "Owe you, my friend. God willing we'll meet again."

"Go make peace with your sister," he says, and I hurry into the storeroom, strap on my Colt and again stuff the LeMats in my belt. I pull on my bearskin coat and head out the back door and turn west in the alley.

When I get out on the street, Hendrick's Mill Road, I see her a half block away, and she walks right past the last house and takes a path along the road.

I wonder where the Hell she's off to, then remember I'd passed the place that had been mentioned to me. Hoys Tea House and Heavenly Pleasures. A Celestial saloon and dope den. In many mining towns, including Bannack City, I'd guess as I saw no Chinee in Holland's, Chinese nor Indians are allowed admission or to wander the streets after dark. Hoy's is on the intersection of the trail coming up from Idaho and the road leading on to the Big Hole, well out of town.

Knowing it to be at least a mile out of town and that I'll have plenty of time to catch up, I head for the livery, pay up the half dollar I owe, saddle up Rusty and lead Roan out of town on her tail.

After no more than a quarter mile, I rein up beside her.

"Ma'am, I got an extra mount here should you prefer to ride?"

She glances over and stares at me as she is striding along, then trips and goes to her knees. She cries out when she puts both hands down to break her fall.

I leap off Rusty and help her to her feet. "You alright?"

"I'm fine. I've had some trouble with my hands and they bother me at times."

"I shouldn't have distracted you, Sarah. I'm sorry."

We stand eying each other for a moment, me expecting her recognition, her wondering who the Hell I am.

Finally, she speaks up. "Do I know you, sir?"

Chapter Ten

Finally, I'm truly eye-to-eye with the sister I thought dead, only to find out I was wrong. A sister I've been searching for nigh a year. And it seems she doesn't recognize me. Possibly…probably…too much opium soaking her brain.

"I should hope so, I'm your brother, Tag." She stares at me, trying to make sense of me standing in front of her.

"Tag died in the war. Besides…,"

I can see she's still affected by the demon smoke as she's speaking slowly with deliberation, "…besides, you're too old to be my brother Tag."

That makes me laugh. "Damn, if we could all stay young that would be something."

She studies me for a moment. "You laugh like Tag."

"Sarah, I am Tag, and I didn't die in the war and had no idea you thought so. When I came home mama had passed, you'd married, and run off with Jake."

Now she really looks confused. Finally, she asks, "Okay, smarty, if you're my brother what's your first name?"

"Rufus, but don't you tell a damn soul. You know I always hated that name."

Her mouth falls open, then she throws her arms around me, and begins to sob. I feel as if a mine-ore car has been lifted off my shoulders.

She pushes away, holds me at arm length, and asks, "Where have you been these ten years or more?"

"My head was not right when I came out of that blood and gore. I was in the high mountains for over five years until I heard of your...your unfortunate trouble. I packed up and went to Nemesis, thinking you dead, finding your family shot down by a pack of lowlife dogs."

"I was...not dead."

She says it as if I can't see the fact.

Then she continues, slowly and methodically. "I've not stopped...mourning my beautiful girls and Jake. But I've many times...wished...I was dead. Wished I could go...go back to Nemesis and...re-venge my girls."

"Too late."

"Too...too late?" She again seems confused.

"I took that chore on myself. All those who came to your home that day, and that no-account Sheriff Tobias Wentworth, and Colonel Mace Dillon...all in

Hell, I hope."

"All of them?"

"Willy Stark, Tate Jorgensen, the Indian Crooked Arm, Liam Toole, Enrico Zaragosa…all but Dillon's nephew, Seth. I spared him as he was but a whelp. He showed remorse and I believed he tried to subvert the others' intentions."

"All dead?" she asks again.

"By my own hand."

We've tarried here too long. So, I ask, "How about you mounting up. I know you can ride like a man, so fork this gray of mine. I'll mount the roan and we'll get the Hell out of here."

She's dead silent for a moment, then turns and starts walking again. "I have to go to Hoy's."

"To fill your pipe?" I ask, talking to her back.

She doesn't answer, so I mount Rusty and rein up beside her again. "It's faster if we ride. We can get what you need, if you have to have it, then ride on."

"I can't leave Will. He's going to take me to Virginia City, then to Helena, then to Fort Benton and pay for my fare as far as St. Louis."

"Sarah, you're wanted by the law…as am I…so we need to move on. I have a place in the mountains where we can lay low until they forget about us."

She strides on. Seemingly thinking about what I'd said, then she surprises me with, "I'm not in trouble with the law. Am I?"

"You killed a man over in Silver Valley—at least that's what the poster on you says."

Again, she seems in deep thought as she strides. "I remember. He tried...tried to do things to me. Things I didn't want to do. He beat me until I thought I was going to die. He held a knife to me. But he sat it down when he was...was distracted. I picked it up."

"And stuck it between his ribs."

She looks up at me, for the first time, fearful. "Are you here...to take me back? Who are you really?"

It's becoming clear to me that she's worse off than I'd feared. If she won't go willingly with me, she'll go, none-the-less.

I guess I'll have to play a new game. "Sarah, Hoy sent me to pick you up so you could hurry along. Will needs you to get back to the room and tend to him."

She glances over, then stops and walks around the roan and tries to get a foot in the stirrup but is having trouble. I dismount and put hands on her narrow waist and give her a boost.

Before I can remount, she's given heels to the roan and is pounding trail.

But I know exactly where she's going as she's in the clutches of the evil smoke.

I close the distance and rein up beside her as she dismounts and runs for the red door of Hoy's Tea and Heavenly Pleasures saloon and dope den. I notice in small letters on his sign, SUPPLIES, so he caters to travelers and those closer to him than town, as well as those who want to drink and whore.

There's a single-up buckboard parked near the several cords of wood and a corral behind the place with two mules and a pinto horse, in addition to six horses and one riding mule tied at the hitching rail.

I'm only steps behind her as she negotiates the doorway.

All heads turn to us as Sarah crashes though the door and I follow, and close it softly behind. It takes a moment for my eyes to adjust, but when they do I wonder how welcome I am as they stare but then go back to drinks and games and conversation.

The place is dark, not unlike a hundred other saloons, except for the mixture of Chinese and whites. Three white men are spaced around, as well as a half a dozen Orientals. Three of the Chinees are at one table playing some kind of board game, two standing talking to two Chinee girls in silk gowns, but with straight skirts and low-cut bodices over small breasts. The one in the red silk is a decent looking lass, with perfect golden skin, the other a bit rough with skin that resembles a walnut. They both have a generous head of black hair, and both heads are adorned with large tortoise shell combs.

The furnishings are bare, a plank bar, tables with a variety of ladder back and Windsor turned-spindles chairs, none of which match, and wood crates used for seating. I've been in higher class joints.

The sixth Oriental is behind the bar. A potbellied man in a black silk shirt and a miner's canvass trousers. His pants are held up by a wide black belt, which keeps an Arkansas toothpick as long as his forearm close under the belly. All the Chinese men have queues to the middle of their backs, including him. Only one of them is heeled, and I'm surprised at that as it's common for Celestials to be denied firearms in many parts of the West.

Sarah moves straight to the bar in the dimly lit room.

"Ah, Miss Sarah," the bartender greets her. "Where is my good friend Will?"

"He's under the weather. He says you owe him and I came to pick up two ounces."

"And who might your friend be?" he asks.

Chapter Eleven

She turns back and eyes me as if she's never seen me before. "Don't worry about him. I need those two ounces."

"Miss Sarah, if Mr. Will Dougle here, I would—"

"Wait," she digs into the reticula, the small bag hung from her wrist, and comes up with a five-dollar gold piece. "A dollar an ounce. Give me five."

He moves to a cabinet behind the bar and comes back with a small tin, the size of a snuff box. She grabs it up quickly and moves to the rear of the place, finds a table away from others, pulls a glass pipe from her reticule, loads it, then reaches for another small case. Sheremoves and sweeps a Lucifer across its side and heats it until the sap begins to simmer and smoke. She draws deeply on its glass stem.

In moments, her face goes slack as she leans back in the chair—now the picture of contentment.

I'm standing at the front of the place, my gaze shifting from her to the man behind the bar, whom I presume is Hoy, to the other gents in the place and back to her.

As the bartender is eying me like I might be the law, I move over to the bar, extend my hand, "Talbot. And you are."

"Hoy. This place mine."

"Congratulations. You got rye whiskey?"

"You got two bits?" he asks.

"The bottle?"

"Four fingers, that glass," he points.

"For an honest pour of whiskey that ain't been watered down."

He turns to the back bar, also constructed of rough sawn planks, and pulls a label-less bottle down from a shelf and pours me four fingers of whatever rot gut he's serving. Hoping I'm not going to go blind, I take it in two gulps and place four bits on the bar. "Another, please."

He smiles and pours this one to the brim—at least five fingers. "I may have another after I chat with the lady."

"Pretty one dollar a poke. Other one six bits."

I nod, head their way, but pass them, go to the back and pull up a chair next to Sarah. She's leaning back, puffing slowly on her pipe.

"Are you ready to go?" I ask.

"Wha…" she manages, without opening her eyes.

"Go. How about we go?"

"Wha…" she mumbles again.

"Who you?" The voice rings over my shoulder and I turn to see Hoy close behind me.

"Mr. Dougle is under the weather and assigned me to watch over Miss Sarah."

"I not know you. When you come Bannack City?"

I rest my hand on the Colt on my belt, and eye him like a bull at a bastard calf. "Look, friend, I'm taking care of Miss Sarah. You want to fetch me another whiskey, do so. Otherwise keep out of my business and don't slip up on my backside. You'll find your-self being shipped home covered in charcoal and salt, you're not careful."

But he's not easily dissuaded and his hand rests on the hilt of the Arkansas toothpick. "When you come Bannack City? I no know you. I never see you with Dougle."

I stand slowly, watching carefully as his hand tightens on the hilt.

"Mr. Hoy, unless that pig sticker holds six or more rounds, you're about to get an expensive lesson in running a drinking establishment. Some customers take umbrage at being insulted and I'm first on that list. I'm taking care of Miss Sarah. You get me an-other whiskey or get your ass out to shovel out the corral. I don't give a tinker's damn."

I lift the Colt an inch. He doesn't look a damn bit fearful but does spin on his heel and head back to the bar.

I turn back to Sarah, and ask again, "Sarah, I need to get you out of here. Can you walk?"

Hoy is back quickly with the bottle, and pours me another, but he looks like a snake eying a rat.

"That your wagon outside?" I ask.

"Yes, my wagon. Get supplies. Get wood."

"Is it for sale?" If I know Celestials, everything is for sale for the right price.

"I just buy. I pay thirty five dollars. Then work, work, work on wagon."

"You got robbed. It's still a wreck."

He shrugs. "I have wagon. You want wagon. You have sixty dollars you own wagon."

"Forty."

"Sixty.

"Forty-five, last offer."

He shrugs again. "Sixty."

"Fifty-five and you throw in one of those mules."

"Fifty-five and you don't pay last whisky."

"Fifty-five, don't pay whiskey, you throw in tack for one horse." Hoy nods agreement.

"You got any blankets," I ask.

"Have many. Things for sale in storeroom."

"How much?"

"Dollar for fine thick wool Hudson."

"Here's a fifty-dollar gold piece and another ten. Load five new Hudson blankets in the back of the buckboard. Make sure—fine, thick, clean, and new blankets. I'm gonna fetch a horse."

I head out to the front, lead Roan around and drop his saddle and the bags in the back as Hoy comes out a side door and throws the blankets in. I spread them to make a bed, and check the reins and traces and am not happy. But as Hoy's is anything but a saddlery, I take what I can get. I have no idea if Roan has ever pulled a wagon, but as I'm going to lead him I imagine it will be of little consequence.

He stands easy in the traces and collar, and that's a good thing.

Before I return for Sarah I pull the coach gun from its scabbard on Roan's saddle, and lay it in the seat of the buckboard.

I move in through the side door and find myself at the rear of the saloon. Sarah still leaning quietly back in her ladder back chair against the wall, only occasionally lifting the pipe for a small pull, never opening her eyes.

Hoy is watching me carefully, and when I pick her up and head for the door, he jogs my way, yelling something at others in the room.

Luckily I have her laid in the back of the buckboard when he busts out followed by two other Orientals, one of them armed and pulling his revolver from a sash he wears around his waist.

I'm standing on the far side of the buckboard away from them, my hand on the coach gun which they can't see in the wagon's seat.

"Where you take her?" How snaps.

"Back to Mr. Dougle, of course. She can't ride."

"I think I send Hong Lee to Mr. Dougle. You wait."

The armed Chinee is pulling the revolver slowly from his sash, but not nearly fast enough. I lift the scatter gun and cock both barrels as I swing it on them.

There's something about the cocking of both barrels on a scatter gun that commands attention.

The one reaching for the revolver quickly abandons the idea and has both hands, palm out, as he backs for the door. The other unarmed one turns, runs and rounds the back corner of the saloon.

Hoy, to his credit, stands with hands on hips, glaring at me.

"You ain't real smart for a Chinaman," I say in something less than a friendly tone.

"You go straight to town with Miss Sarah," he commands.

I walk to the back of the wagon, never taking the muzzles off of Hoy. When I get clear of the wagon, it's my turn to command. "You get your heathen ass back in the saloon and don't stick your head out or I'll blow it into chunks no bigger than that rice you shovel into your gut."

He doesn't move, so I drop the muzzle and blow

a hole the size of his head in the dirt near his feet. After he lights from jumping two feet straight up, he moves, and I don't think his feet hit twice in the near twenty feet between him and the side door.

I quickly mount Rusty, and lead the roan and wagon out to the road, but don't turn toward Bannack City. Rather I head toward the Big Hole.

I know the road, a decent two-track on the west side of the Big Hole, down into the Bitterroot Valley. From there I can find my way back into the Selway from Salmon Trading Post up until the Salmon can damn near be leapt, and will. With luck, my old log hideout in the high lonely will be vacant. If no one has stumbled on it and decided to take advantage of my five years of improvements.

And if I don't get ridden down by Dougle and his friends or by some other owlhoots trying to collect the three hundred dollars on my head.

And if my own sister doesn't awaken and try to take my head off.

Or doesn't have such a need when has the lack of it, that she murders me in my sleep to get away. As she's had the last of it when those five ounces she bought are smoked up.

And that's a Hell of a lot of what ifs.

But right now it's get clear of Will Dougle before he sic's the law on me, if the law will do his bidding, or before he gets well enough to take to the trail to tack my hide to the outhouse wall. He likely won't get close enough again for me to smash his thick nose with my hard head.

He's not the kind of man to let a little bump on the head keep him down for long. Now I kinda wish I'd hit him hard enough to send him to Hell.

Cause I'm pretty sure that's where he'd like to see me.

Chapter Twelve

We are an hour on the trail before Sarah comes to, sits up in the back of the buckboard, and hits me on the back with the flat of her hand.

"Where's my smoke?" she asks, without bothering with "where the Hell are we" or "where the Hell are we going."

I turn and over my shoulder invite her. "Would you like to join me up here?"

"I remember…Tag. Where are you taking me? Where's my smoke?"

"You've got four and a half ounces left. It's in the jockey box under my feet, along with your pipe and that silly little firebox."

"I need it."

"You sure as Hell don't need it, but if that's all that will make you happy, I'll dig it out for you."

"Do it."

"That stuff doesn't make a body real polite, does it?"

"Do it, please."

"Climb up front with me and you can dig it out. I want to get some road behind us."

She rises and I worry about her tumbling out of the buckboard to the road, but she manages to get one leg over the seat back, then the other, and promptly bends to get in the jockey box. She slaps my legs so I'd raise them, opens the flap-door and finds her pipe, her little fire box, and box of Lucifers. In minutes she has the demon smoke rising from the sap and is drawing deeply on the pipe, which is a device that has to be heated from the bottom to turn the sap to smoking. When she's taken three deep draws, she turns to me.

"You're going toward the setting sun. That's west. Bannack City is east of Hoy's. Are you lost?"

"No, Sarah. I'm taking you away from that life."

"But, Will?"

Knowing how dependent she is on the evil smoke, I've decided deception is the only way to get her shed of Dougle and, hopefully, eventually, the opium.

"To Hell with Will. I'm taking you to my place."

"But, who'll—"

"I grow my own. I have an acre of poppies at my place. Buckets full of that wonderful sap you like."

"Need. I need it. I have to have it. I don't like it, but I have to have it. I mean, I do like it. I love it but I hate it. But I have to have it."

She's talking gibberish. "There will be all you

want, as often as you want." I'm getting pretty good at lying, as I've been doing so as long as I've been hunting my sis. And my sis is so totally confused by the demon smoke, she's easy to lie to.

Without a word, she, seeming satisfied with my lie, climbs back into the bed of the buckboard, rolls up in the blankets, and with her eyes closed, draws on the pipe until sleep or unconsciousness takes her to Celestial heaven.

We are well into the deep grass meadows of Big Hole when I decide I must stop and rest the stock. We passed a trading post with a sign announcing it to be Jackson, and a woman peeked out the window, but I didn't slow and she didn't yell a welcome or an invitation to come in. So, I make another mile in the darkness, with only a rising moon and stars to light my chores. After I unharness and hobble the stock in belly deep but drying grass, we camp on the banks of its small river. We have miles of grassland in the Hole's nearly flat bottom to cross before we climb to the divide—actually a high pass—between the head-waters of the Bitterroot River to the north and the Salmon to the south. We'll find a better wagon road there, and if the law or Dougle don't catch up and make a fight of it before, we'll head to the Salmon, then abandon the wagon or sell it to an old friend who I hope still runs the place and follow the stream upriver into the Selway, and my old home place.

If it still stands and has not been purloined by others.

I take my bedroll under the wagon and Sarah has the wagon bed. I hear her strike another Lucifer and see it's flare in the middle of the night. At this rate she'll be out of smoke in two days or so. Thank the good Lord for small favors.

Then, I imagine, we'll be past the divide and dropping into the Salmon River valley.

I won't be surprised that things will get lots tougher when she runs out of the false pleasure the smoke brings her. Lots and lots tougher.

***

On the third morning after being clubbed down, Will Dougle dresses and leaves the room. He has no idea where Sarah has gone and really doesn't much give a damn. He does, however, give a damn about evening the score with the scum who'd beat him to the floor.

That did his reputation no good. He was considering staying around Bannack City and maybe even running for Sheriff, knowing the current Sheriff is unpopular with the saloon operators and the miners.

Now that likely won't happen as he's been embarrassed by a man a half head shorter than he and forty or more pounds lighter.

He walks on to Matia's and enters and climbs on

a stool at the counter. Like lunch and dinner, Matia serves everyone the same fare. This morning it is mush, biscuits, fried trout, and a couple of cackleberries to the customer's taste. And coffee of course. It is the only meal that Matia doesn't accompany with rich red wine.

The Basque proprietor exits the kitchen with coffee pot in one hand and four cups hanging from the fingers of the other.

Dougle frowns at him, taps the counter impatiently, and Matia places a cup and pours it to the brim. He eyes Dougle and can hardly hide the smile but tries. Then he says, "Looks like the swelling has gone down. You can breathe all right through that snouse?"

Dougle makes a low sound like a dog growling at an intruder, then clears his throat. "Don't you worry about it. You seen Sarah about?"

"Day before yesterday, hoofing it on by likely heading out to Hoy's."

Dougle shakes his head knowingly, then snaps, "Feed me."

"Who was that little fella you tangled with? The talk of the town it is." Matia knows well that the fella calling himself Talbot is average size in fact a little bigger than most, but he can't help but dig Dougle a little.

"He weren't so little, and he hit me from behind.

He'll get his come-uppins."

"From behind eh?" Again, Matia smiles. "Damn hard to head butt a fella on the nose from behind."

"God dammit, Etcheverry, are you gonna feed me some of that slop you serve, or stand there and jaw? You could find yourself wearing one of those cast iron pots of your'n, you're not careful."

Matia grins as he returns to the kitchen.

An hour and a half later, Dougle reins up in front of Hoy's and dismounts as a man rides in from the west and ties up at the other end of the rail. The fella is riding a black horse of at least sixteen hands and single foots the animal the last hundred feet to the rail; one fist on his side as if he's riding in a Washington D.C. parade. A general leading his troop to be reviewed by President Grant. He dismounts, throws a quick circle of rein on the rail, pulls a comb from his saddlebag and slicks his hair, beats the dust from his clothes with his hat, then slips a neckerchief from a pocket and walks to the front stoop and cleans his boots.

He looks over at Dougle, who is studying him without moving away from his animal.

Dougle is a bit amused at the popinjay, but the man is at least as large as Dougle and is well heeled with a nickel-plated revolver and a belt full of cartridges. So he doesn't laugh out loud.

The man gives Dougle a nod, folds his neckerchief

carefully, pockets it and pushes his way into Hoy's.

Dougle follows twenty feet behind and tracks the man to the plank bar where Hoy is already serving the man a cup of tea.

Leaning on the planks six feet from the man, Dougle continues to eye him. After a sip the man turns to him.

"You got some kind of problem with me, pilgrim?" he asks.

Dougle chuckles, then snorts through his swollen nose. "Hell, I got no problem with no one."

"By the looks of your olfactory organ, you had some trouble with someone. You tickle your mule's heel?"

Dougle ignores him. He is in no condition to trade blows with anyone, much less someone his own size. Instead he turns to Hoy."

"You seen Sarah about? Last I heard she was headed this way, and I'm missing five dollars in gold from my poke."

"Fella here take Sarah two day ago. That way," he motions with a movement of his head to the west. "I raise Hell, but he shoot at me."

"What fella?" Dougle snaps.

"Never see before. But he buy wagon and Miss Sarah leave in back of buckboard."

"He bought that old beat up buckboard and ratty harness from you? Damn fool."

"He damn lucky I no kill. He 'most blew my foot off with scattergun. Had a Colt and LeMats and—"

"LeMats?" Rollie O'Bannon interrupts.

"Yes," Hoy nods, then adds, "Winchester, scattergun, Colt, and LeMats. I think one more LeMat in saddle holster."

"Give me a whisky," Dougle snarls, "and don't think I'm paying. You owe me."

Hoy shrugs, as O'Bannon pulls a folded poster from his pocket and flattens it on the planks. "I don't guess this could be that fella?"

Hoy studies it as he over pours Dougle's glass all the way to the rim. Dougle quickly picks it up and sucks down a half inch, then moves closer and he, too, studies the poster.

The he growls, "That could be the som' bitch what sneaked up and clubbed me while I was playin' cards."

Hoy shrugs, but says, "If had guess, say maybe, for sure."

O'Bannon chuckles. "Maybe for sure? You'd make a fine witness."

Dougle turns to face O'Bannon. "You a law dog?"

"No, sir. I do collect a bounty now and again."

Dougle sticks his hand out and O'Bannon shakes with him. Then Dougle asks, "How far does a bounty hunter ride for three hundred?"

O'Bannon gives him a tight smile and a nod. "Far

as it takes, I guess."

"You think this fella is the one rode out of here with my lady?"

"No idea, but I mean to find out." Then he turns to Hoy, "How long ago did you say they left in a buckboard?"

"Two and half days. Ride northwest Big Hole way."

O'Bannon turns to Dougle again. "You on your way back to Bannack City?"

"I am, but just to load up with some supplies. No one takes a woman from me. Besides she stole five dollars and I mean to make both them pay."

"Tell you what," O'Bannon says, studying Dougle, "You ride with me and I'll split that three hundred with you. If it's my man, and by all that's holy, it sure sounds like him to me." He buries a smile as this Dougle fella has no way of knowing the bounty is now two thousand.

"And I get to shoot the som'bitch and take the woman, should I want her?" Dougle says.

"Fine with me, pilgrim," O'Bannon says, but is lying through his teeth. If this is the woman he thinks it is, she's worth another five hundred. He'll be happy to pay this Dougle fella a hundred and a half or a half ounce of hot lead, after they catch up with McBain and the woman.

But he'll worry about that later.

"You go back to town," he says to Dougle and hands him a five dollar gold piece. "Coffee and a full slab of pork belly, two pounds of hardtack. And make sure you tell the law, or leave word if there's no law about, that O'Bannon headed west...or northwest or wherever the Hell Big Hole is. And bring me the change and don't get hornswoggled. Got it?"

Dougle looks him up and down, then replies, "I got it, O'Bannon, but I don't take orders I give 'em."

O'Bannon gives him a tight grin in return, then snaps, "You know this Big Hole country?"

"Never been there."

"Then, sir, I'm the professional bounty hunter. Read this." He digs in his shirt pocket and pulls out the Leslie's Weekly article he is never without.

Dougle reads, then pales a little. "You're that O'Bannon."

"One and the same. You ride with me you take orders. Or I'll bring them in alone and you can have the hindmost."

Dougle shrugs, and nods. "Looks like you know your business. I'll ride along. One fifty and the woman is mine, we ride them down?" Dougle thinks about it, and smothers a smile. He can get his revenge and make a hundred fifty doing it—and maybe three hundred if this big bounty hunter turns his back on him after they get their prey in chains.

O'Bannon continues. "Go to town, leave the law

my message, bring back your supplies and fill my order. You'll eat outta your saddlebags and me outta mine. Take my lead and we'll have them, in chains or dead, inside a week and you'll soon have your money."

Dougle nods and downs the rest of his whiskey, spins on his heel and heads for the door.

Chapter Thirteen

We ride in easy company with each other. Sarah awakes, smokes and sinks into oblivion again. Had I not forced her to eat, making soup from jerky and what wild onions and watercress I could pick, she'd not have worried about a bite and only occasionally a sip of water.

She is killing herself and happy with the trip.

While pulling up a slight rise, I see we are going to come on a fella, all alone, hands on his hips, staring at a wagon with a rear wheel off, it flat in the road.

Two substantial mules and a fine sorrel horse are hobbled in the grass not far from the wagon.

The wagon is a fairly good-sized freight wagon, a Studebaker I'd guess, covered with a fine white canvas and painted in letters. As I near I can read, SUPERIOR FARM IMPLEMENTS and below that in smaller letters, ALEX ENGSTROM, REPRE-SENTATIVE. I rein up.

"How do you do, Mr. Engstrom, fancy seeing you again."

"Well, thank the good Lord. Mr. Talbot, or should I say Captain Talbot?"

"Mister will do fine. Hunter in fact. It seems you've got a little trouble."

"Damned if someone didn't steal my axle jack from hanging under my wagon. I didn't notice it was gone until I needed it. I don't imagine—"

"No jack, but you and I can find us a pry bar—a good limb will do—and get her up on another chunk of log to hold her while you get that wheel back in place. Did you find the hub nut?"

"Had to backtrack afoot a quarter mile, but she was laying right in the center of the road."

He walks over next to my wagon and stares down at Sarah, then looks at me and takes a step back. "She dead?"

I have to smile, but tightly. "Nope, trying to kill herself with the Celestial pleasure, but I'm soon to break her of it. But not until I get her somewhere she can't hurt herself or me."

"Pity. Fine looking woman, I'd guess. Your wife?"

"Sister. You keep watch in case she comes around. I'll take my saddle horse and ride to that timber up ahead. You got an ax and a crosscut?"

"Finest. That's my business. I'll dig them out. I see you have a lariat. You can drag something back. But it's my problem. Sure you don't want me—"

"I can handle it. Keep watch. I had a little trouble

back in Bannack City and there may be some fellas on my tail, so I'm not wasting any time."

With that I dismount the buckboard, hurry to the back with my Winchester in hand and shove it into Rusty's saddle scabbard. I untie him, suck up his latigo which I'd left looser than normal, ride up to the rear of Alex's wagon and grab the ax and crosscut he hands me.

Gigging Rusty away we gallop a little over a half mile until we're past the meadows and in the timber at the west edge of the Big Hole. I pull rein in a stand of lodge pole pine with lots of downfall. Dismounting where I have two dozen downed trees to choose from I soon locate a fairly fresh tree with little rot, knock the braches off, cut a twelve foot length of six inch diameter timber, rope it, and we are off.

Dragging it at a canter as I near I yell to Alex, who's busy unloading various heavy items from the rear of the wagon to lighten our lift. "Free it and I'll go cut us a chunk to put under the axel."

"I'd say you got more than we need. Let's cut the right length off the fat end."

And he is right. We soon have a twenty-inch length sawed flat on each end, the pry log under the rear axel, and with the two of us, manage to pry it up. I hold it while he fits the short log under the axel then the wheel back in plac, and I'm able to let off and suck some deep breaths.

Quickly he applies some fresh grease to the axel. He has the proper nut wrench, and in less than a minute is ready to get back on the road. But first I help him reload some heavy iron, mostly small but heavy cases of plow shears and harrow teeth.

Sarah hasn't moved a muscle.

"It'll be dark in an hour," Alex says, wiping sweat from his brow with a backhand. "I'd like to ride along and fix y'all a fine supper, if you have a mind to. Seems I owe you at least that."

"We've got to rest, and who knows what the road holds ahead. Likely something I'd not like to face in the dark. I'd be obliged."

"Beans have been soaking for a full day, I have a sack of apples, potatoes and carrots, and a haunch of antelope. And cooking for three will give me an excuse to break out my Dutch oven and show off my apple cobbler."

"A damn sight better than my jerky and hardtack. Let's go," I said, with a wide smile. "I'll lead out and ride until I find a place we can get off the road. If I'm being pursued it's likely they'll be catching up with me tomorrow or the next day."

I welcomed the company. Sarah had been about as much company as a boil on my butt. But I had her and would soon have her on the comeback trail.

I knew it would take most of a week, if not more, after she had no more sap to reach for, and it would likely be pure Hell.

But it had been a long trail, and if she wasn't only a hull of her former self, the self I knew from over ten years past, it was well worth the trek and would be worth the grief I'd receive while she was getting shed of the dragon who gnawed at her insides.

If we'd manage to fight shy of those who were likely on our tail.

Chapter Fourteen

In the first copse of fir we'd seen since pulling up a long gentle rise out of the grassland that's the Big Hole, I find a trickle of water and turn south until we're fairly well out of sight of the two-track wagon road. I'm pleased to be camping with Alex as he pulls his larger wagon up a dozen feet from and beside the buckboard, grabs up a canvas from the back of his and makes us a cover that'll keep us out of the weather by stretching it between the two.

In a few minutes, while I'm getting Sarah on her feet, he's fetched water, has a kettle and Dutch oven hanging over a modest camp fire, and, glory be, has broken out a bottle of Southern Star bourbon.

Alex and I sip while he chops carrots, potatoes, and antelope hindquarter, then adds it to the fresh creek water in one of his cast iron Dutch ovens. In a second smaller one he cooks biscuits, then when they're done sets them aside and starts a cobbler from the apples topped with the same dough he used for biscuits, generously dusted with sugar.

Sarah has given him a strange look, not bothered to ask who he is or where he came from but has wandered off into the nearby woods to take care of her needs.

I'm encouraged by the fact she returns, asks for a cloth and borrows a comb from Alex, the moves away again so she can get some privacy away from camp and clean up.

It's chilly, but she doesn't seem to mind. She returns with her hair combed and looking far better than she has since we left Hoy's. But still she fills her pipe and smokes a little before supper is served. And she eats something well before she finishes the pipe. I'm glad to see she's down to an ounce of sap. Tomorrow will be the true test of getting her weaned of the demon.

Alex is not through with his chores. I take the Dutch ovens and tins to the trickle of water and use some sand grit to scrub them clean. He uses a chunk of fat he's cut from the haunch to oil the larger Dutch oven then greases and fills the smaller with beans and a chunk of fatback and sets it right down on the edge of the fire. He gives me a grin, "Breakfast," he says.

"By all that's holy," I say, "If you had the proper equipment I'd ask you to marry."

He laughs. "A fella on the road alone has got to learn to take care of himself."

I make Sarah a bed of her five blankets near

enough to the fire that she'll get some warmth. Alex retires to the back of his wagon, and I roll out my bedroll in the back of the buckboard.

There's adequate graze along the creek so I've hobbled my stock as Alex has done. Graze and water for the animals, my gut stuffed with the finest meal I've had since Matia's, and Sarah sleeping quiet—even if it's with the help of poison smoke.

I'm content, for the moment, even if the fact there's likely someone on my trail wanting to ventilate my hide.

Not being a man lately taken to prayer, as I fear the man upstairs might be a little angry with my taking revenge on a half-dozen of his children during my time in Nemesis, I take the chance to make a small request. "Lord, let me get this lady who's fallen on hard times safely away from them who've used her badly and poisoned her with that demon smoke. For most the years I've had the pleasure to know her, she's been faithful to your word. I'd be obliged. Amen." The earth doesn't shake nor the sky roar and bolt, so I guess my asking hasn't offended.

I sleep as if I've been riding hard for five days without, and awaken to Alex stirring the fire and heating beans and biscuits.

As soon as I sit up, he shushes me.

"What?" I say, softly.

"A couple of riders passed a few minutes ago.

They got an early start or camped not far back."

"Going which way?" I ask.

"Same as us. If they're hunting you, even in pre-dawn light, I'd think they'd see the wagon track leaving the road."

"I should have swept it out," I say, cussing myself.

"I want to go back to Bannack City," Sarah says, sitting up in her blankets.

"You're not going back," I say, a little sting in my voice.

"But...but I'll be out of the pleasure by the end of today. Even as it is I'd be suffering badly before we get back to Hoy or Will if we started back this moment."

Time to lie again. "I told you, I have an acre of poppies and a gallon of sap, not far away."

"You're not lying to me are you, Tag."

"Tag?" Alex askes. "I thought your name was Hunter."

I smile at him. "Childhood nickname."

He nods, but I'm thinking he's tied her comment to the posters—two of which we've seen and I've stopped and torn from trees since leaving Hoy's. That was before we tied up with Alex and I can only hope he didn't bother to rein his wagon up and read "Taggart McBain."

We take our time getting his mules and Roan into harness and his horse and Rusty tied on to trail.

When we're ready to set out, he turns to me. "Hunter, or whatever your name truly is, I have long been sure the law is not always in the right. I don't care what trouble you may have recently had. You treated me fairly during the war and been fair since we met back up. And you didn't have to stop and help with that wheel. That said, I won't join you in a fight with lawmen. You understand?"

"Let's hope it doesn't come to that," I say, without admitting anything. "You said you're going north to St. Mary's in the Bitterroot Valley and we'll be turning south to Salmon Trading Post. If you'd prefer, I'll head out ahead of you so it's clear we're not acquainted. The Salmon Bitterroot road can't be more than ten or fifteen miles ahead and we'll part ways there nonetheless."

"Then we might as well train up until we part ways."

So we set out.

As soon as we're back on the road, I can see two horsebackers have recently passed.

One of the horses has a nick in its rear right-side shoe, not that it tells me anything other than that. But should it be on my trail again, I'll know it's the same critter.

Now I don't know if my pursuers are ahead or behind, and I wonder how long it will be, if ahead, when they realize the wagon wheel track they've been following is no longer in their path.

If so, they'll likely turn back.

So, I take up the lead, both LeMats fully loaded including a twenty-guage shotshell full of cut-up square nails, my coach gun with the same type loads only twelve gauge, my Colt, and my Winchester. I want to see them coming and be ready for them; and I damn sure am as ready as I can get.

The Hell of it is my sis is pretty damn exposed in the rear of the wagon—even prone on the floor-boards.

It would be a terrible twist of fate to get her killed after all I've gone through, first to find revenge for her and her family then to find her and get her under my wing.

Chapter Fifteen

———————————

The Pollock brothers have ridden hard to arrive in Bannack City and caught up on their drinking in Holland's.

They awake with bad heads, their bed rolls under the heavy boughs of a fir tree a hundred yards up the hill from Hendrick's Mill Road, the town's main street.

Arlo sits up and bumps his head on a low branch, knocking trash down the back of his shirt.

"Son of a bitch." He pulls his shirt off and brushes the trash off his back the best he can, then throws his cover off and gives his brother a sharp kick, awakening him.

"Gol dang it, Arlo, what was that for?"

"Fer being ugly and sleepin' too long. I'm gonna roll up and see if that saloon is open yet and get me some hair of the ol' dog. My head feels like a couple of big horns have gone to buttin' between my ears."

"Let's go," Jethro says, and uncovers and rolls up.

Their horses are staked nearby, in some sparse

grass they'd munched clean, so they were quickly saddled and rode a quarter mile. The little town is coming awake with the barber and the owner of the mercantile both sweeping off the boardwalks in front of their establishment. Matia Etcheverry is unlocking the front door to Good Eats. But whoever runs Hollands has yet to put in an appearance.

The Pollocks tie up in front of the saloon and dismount.

"You wanna go get some chow?" Jethro asks as they mount the boardwalk and peer into the window panes next to Holland's batwing doors.

"Naw," Arlo grumbles. "We ain't got much coin left. That rot gut they pour in this place got me sick as a poisoned pup. I need a shot or two of good whiskey to settle the worms a'fore I try and fill the void with flapjacks."

"Good luck. Ain't a soul about. If you hadn't a drank a quart, you'd likely feel some better."

"Shudup. Let's take a look around back."

Jethro shrugs and follows his brother down a four-foot space between buildings and they mount the boardwalk between the saloon and a privy farther out back a few steps. Arlo jerks on the door and it gives a little.

"Ain't much of a door or lock," he says, looking up and down the alley to make sure no one's about.

Jethro shakes his head. "We got a little coin left,

Arlo, we don't need to be—"

"We ain't got enough," Arlo snaps, before Jethro can finish. Then Arlo pulls back a booted foot gives the door its heel so hard the planks splinter, then kicks it again until he can pass through.

He turns to his brother. "That weren't so tough. I'm gonna find where they hide the good whiskey, and maybe some coin." He stoops and forces his way between splintered planks.

"Piss poor idea," Jethro says, but follows.

They move inside and down a hallway to the bar and go behind and Arlo soon has a bottle of labeled whiskey and is pouring two coffee mugs full.

He downs the first mug full and gives his brother a grin. "Poor idea?"

"A little better now," Jethro says, returning the grin.

They've downed two mugs each and are half into the third, when they hear the double doors that cover the batwings on the outside being unlocked.

"Let's go," Jethro snaps, and starts to the rear.

"Hell with it," Arlo says, and stands his ground.

The man enters not seeing the brothers in the dim light as drapes cover the windows.

He makes a half-dozen steps their way when he stops short. "What the Hell…"

"Come on in," Arlo says, and chuckles. He has his Leech & Rigdon—Confederate copy of the Colt—in hand, and the sound of the heavy revolver cocking rings through the place.

"Hold on there," the man says, holding his left hand out, palm facing Arlo. "You two know who I am?" His other hand clutches a box, painted in an Oriental motif.

"Well, sir, you look a little like Ulysses S. Grant, but I imagine not," Arlo says, and laughs, then winces as his head still hurts. He clears his throat, the snarls, "The fact is, pardner, I don't much give a damn who you are. I do give a damn what's in that pretty little box you're totin'."

"I'm Sean O'Leary, owner of this place, but you should be more interested in the fact I'm currently the appointed Sheriff of Bannack City while our Sheriff is over in Virginia City in a trial. I suggest you lay down that weapon and I'll see you only get a week or so for breaking and entering—"

"What's in the box?" Jethro speaks up from the rear, with enough authority that it echoes through the place.

O'Leary shades his eyes with a hand. "So, there's two of you brigands?" he says.

"Yep, and a half-dozen more outside," Arlo says. "Now, pilgrim, the box."

O'Leary is as tall as Arlo, but not nearly so bulky. He acts as if he's going to hand the box to Arlo but as he moves forward he make sure the big man is between him and the other fellow in the back of the room, more than thirty feet from him.

He extends his right hand and the box, and Arlo, obviously depending upon his brother in the rear, holsters his weapons.

When Arlo reaches for the box, O'Leary lets it fall, and grabs for the little Sheriff's model Colt on his hip.

Arlo is bending to recover the box and O'Leary fires. The big man takes the shot which cuts a groove down his back and reels backward clawing for his holstered weapon.

O'Leary swings his muzzle to the man in the back, more worried about him than the now wounded man and gets a shot off.

But it goes wild as Jethro has dropped to a knee and with both hands on his weapon, and he fires and O'Leary spins away and drops to a knee facing back toward the doors he'd entered. He no more than touches the knee down when he's up and running for the exit.

Jethro is climbing to his feet and fires a quick shot at the fleeing O'Leary, but misses as the man slams through the batwings and turns and runs.

Charging forward, Jethro bends and hooks a hand under Arlo's arm and lifts him. His back is covered with blood. "We gotta go, brother," Jethro says.

"Damn if that don't hurt," Arlo yells, but he's

clamoring to his feet with the help of his brother. "Grab the damn box," he says, and Jethro scoops it up and they head for the front as they've left their horses there.

Jethro helps Arlo into the saddle, then mounts up and they both give heels to the horses and pound out of town to the east. They don't look back as lead whistles around them and shots are fired behind.

"Can you ride?" Jethro yells at his brother.

"What the Hell do you think I'm a'doin'?" Arlo yells back.

"I mean for a distance?" Jethro says.

"Nothing broke, I don't think," Arlo says, but he's grimacing.

"Let's circle around town and head out the other way, now that we're out of sight," Jethro suggests. I was tolt there's a place that'a'way. Choy's or some damn thing. Let them chase us all the way east to Virginia City while we ride west."

In another two hundred yards they come to a four-foot-wide stream crossing the wagon road, and Jethro reins off to the north, upstream, looks back over his shoulder to make sure his brother is following, then hunkers down with willows slapping at him, putting distance between them and the road.

After a mile of hard riding, back west with a hill between them and Bannack City, Arlo yells at his brother, "Too much gol'darn blood. We gotta stop."

Jethro reins off into a copse of trees and jumps from his horse and helps Arlo down. He lifts his shirt and sees the bullet has cut a half inch grove down his shoulder and scapula.

"Hard damn place to patch," Jethro mumbles.

"Get my spare shirt out of my left saddlebag and do yer best. I keep squirting blood like this and you'll be diggin' me a hole."

Jethro guffaws as he digs the shirt out, "And starve all those coyotes and wolves?"

"You got an ass kickin' coming. Patch me up."

Chapter Sixteen

———————————————

It is mid-morning when Rollie O'Bannon and Will Dougle come to the Salmon-St. Mary's road. Now it's choose; north to St. Mary's Mission in the Bitterroot Valley, or south to Salmon. They are perched on the top of a saddle between Salmon and St. Mary's, and ahead is a steep mountain and no road but north or south, either way, is downhill, a two-track, and should be easy riding.

Will dismounts and removes a bottle of whiskey from his saddlebag and takes a deep suck, then backhands the wet from his mouth. "You wanna flip a coin?" he asks the bounty hunter.

"I been thinking. This old road is pretty damn hard, but we should'a been seeing some wagon track that's way more recent than what I observe. Back aways I was seeing what I figure was the track of the buckboard y'all were talking about back at that Hoy's place. And we been seeing another deep track from a heavy loaded wagon. Now neither. You don't suppose we been hornswoggled? Maybe McBain turned off the road, hid out and let us pass? Maybe he waylaid whosoever was driving that heavy wagon and kilt them for the goods."

"Could be," Will says, with a shrug. "That's an old grizzly bear trick—lettin' pursuers pass then followin' up to gnaw their heads off. But, I don't think this fool is that smart. Why don't you ride back and take a gander? I'll just wander over to that big ol' fir tree and have me a nap."

"And you won't see half that three hundred, you don't do your part. McBain's wanted for killing a half-dozen men and I can take him alone. But why take the chance? Where I go, you go. Got it?"

Again, Dougle shrugs and remounts. "Lead out, bounty hunter."

O'Bannon swings his big black gelding back the way they'd come and takes off at a canter.

"Ain't no gol'dang hurry," Dougle says, but gigs his horse and follows.

***

Jethro turns his mount back south when he is sure he is well past Bannack City, and picks up the west bound wagon road just in sight of Hoy's. He lets his brother, who is riding hunched over in the saddle, catch up.

"There be some kind of trading post or saloon or both up ahead. Got a sign but I can't read it from here.

Maybe they got a woman there knows how to doctor better than me."

"A goddamn donkey could doctor better than you. We get up there I'll stay mounted. You go in and check it out and come get me they can be help."

Jethro nods and gives heels to his horse and trots on ahead. He dismounts seeing Hoy's sign, encouraged by no horses at the rail, and decides it would be a place he can at least get a shot of whiskey to keep him fueled to keep up their escape. He now has over seventy dollars in gold and silver in his pocket, thanks to their stopover at Holland's.

He slips the hammer tie off and lifts his Leech and Rigdon slightly so it is loose in the holster then enters.

Two Chinee girls are perched at a table in the back and a Chinese gent stands behind the bar. Jethro strides over and slaps a quarter on the planks. "Whiskey a dime a shot?" he asks.

Hoy nods and reaches under the bar. Jethro rests a hand on the butt of his revolver, and cautions the Chinaman. "I got a fine tongue fulla taste buds. You give me watered hooch and they'll be sending you home in a box."

Hoy merely smiles at him but reaches for a different bottle under the planks and pours a small shot glass up to the rim, a finger more than he would normally have poured without the threat.

Jethro shoots it down his gullet, then asks, "Either of those whores in the back know nursin'?"

"Su Lee fine nurse."

"Give me another bottle of the cheapest you got. Pint will do. I got a man outside needs patching up. We had us a firearm accident."

"Firearm dangerous," Hoy says, knowing the man is lying and also knowing the fastest way to get rid of this sour-smelling man across the bar is to patch his friend up and get them on their way. Then he adds, "Hoy have Su Lee patch up, then you go?"

"You bet. Half dollar for a bottle of that same hooch you poured. And two bits for the pint of the worst you got."

"Four bits and dime for what I pour. Verly good hooch," Hoy says. He doesn't want to barter with this dirty smelly man, but, after all, a dime is a dime.

"Sure, but that includes the doctorin' and dressing."

"Okay, okay. Lay man on porch," he says, then turns and yells at the women in some gibberish Jethro doesn't understand.

Hoy holds out his hand for his money, the bottle in his other hand, but held far enough back Jethro can't reach it.

They trade, Hoy fetches another pint of unlabeled from the back bar, hands it over, and Jethro spins on his heel and heads out.

By the time he has Arlo's shirt and his makeshift dressing off and has him stretched out on Hoy's porch, the women appear. The wound is ugly, a six-inch gouge, but likely not fatal…unless it goes green. One woman carries a tin pan full of hot water and a wash rag, and the other scissors and what looks to be a table cloth, stained but recently washed and pressed.

The first wets the rag then begins to soak the deep gash, which almost immediately begins bleeding again.

Arlo, face down on the boards, growls at the women, "You hurt me, bitch, I hurt you worse—"

"Shudup," Jethro snaps. "Nobody could fix you right without paining you some."

"Some is fine," Arlo mumbles.

"How about this?" Jethro says, and pours a good dollop of the cheap pint into the wound. Arlo jumps but stays down and silent.

Then yells. "Damn, damn, damn, that's another ass kickin' you got coming, Jethro. I'd call you a som'bitch we didn't have the same sainted ma. Give me a swig of that poison."

Jethro hands him the cheap bottle, saving the good for himself, then growls at the women. "Hurry it up. We got to get down the road."

In minutes, they have an eight inch wide dressing tied around Arlo's chest with an extension looped over his shoulder, and Jethro is helping him to his feet, then to mount up.

When Jethro swings a leg over, he turns to the two Chinese girls standing on the porch. "I got a tip for you whores," Jethro says, eliciting a smile from the women. "Get your whorin' asses back to that shithole what sired you."

Now they frown, as Jethro, guffawing, followed by his brother, reins away toward the Big Hole. The ladies hurry back into the saloon. They are happy— even losing a half dollar each they might have made from a poke—that the two smelly men hadn't wanted to go to the cribs in the back.

"What about O'Bannon," Arlo asks as Jethro leads out with his mount at a brisk walk.

"We didn't run into Rollie on the road coming into town, nor in town, nor saw that big black of his'n, so likely he's headed this'a'way. Don't much matter as we gotta get the Hell outta Bannack City, and some damn way the posse likely after us ain't a going."

"Ten miles," Arlo says, with a groan, "then we camp."

"Twenty or more, brother. A dead-set posse is likely to do fifty. You may be hurtin' but not so much as a stretched neck would hurt. Robbin' a Sheriff ain't the smartest thing a Pollock ever did."

"Ride on. I'll keep up."

Chapter Seventeen

The more I drive the buckboard toward the Salm-on-St. Mary's Mission road, the more I'm concerned that the riders who'd passed on the road at dawn were hunting us. Probably Dougle and a helper, or the Bannack City law. Or Hell, maybe a travelling drummer who has no interest in us? But this shouldn't be a common road for sales folk, as many other routes have far more populace.

We are deep into the forest, leaving the grassy plain of the Big Hole behind, when Sarah reaches from her perch in the back of the buckboard and slaps me on the back. "There's only a lousy ounce in my tin. We going to be at your place soon?"

"A day or so. You think you can sit a horse?"

"Of course."

"You suck on that pipe and you can barely sit up. So, stay light on it. Make it last, if you gotta have it at all."

"I have to have it," she says, adamantly.

"We're gonna dump the wagon and go horseback."

"Why? I can't relax and smoke on horseback."

"We can stop when you need a puff or two."

Her jaw was set, and she snaps, "I want to go back to Bannack City and find Will"

It's time I get tough with Sarah. "The Hell if we are going back. We're going on to my place." Then I soften my tone. "Remember, I got an acre of poppies and a gallon or two of sap. And there are some bad people hunting us and we can't evade them in the wagon. So, little sis, it's horseback."

I rein up and Alex is forced to do the same as I lead. I leap from the seat and stride back to stand beside him. "How would you like the gift of a buck-board?"

"What?"

"We're gonna abandon the wagon and go on horseback, and we're gonna leave the road. In fact I'll be needing an ax and something for a bedroll for Sarah. If you'd trade."

"I need another wagon about like I need a dance band—"

"Sell it, first chance you get. It's been good to us so far."

"Well, sir, I hate to lose your company—"

"And we hate to lose your cooking. I hope we'll met again someday. You're a fine friend. Can I help you lash this wagon to trail yours?"

"I guess, if that's your pleasure."

"Not a pleasure I figure a necessity."

While he goes into his wagon for the goods I've requested, I move forward and drive Roan off the road far enough that Alex can pass, then move up behind him. In short order we have the tongues of the buckboard lashed to a point and to the rear of his goods wagon, had saddled Roan, got Sarah situated in the saddle and said our goodbyes to Alex.

My bedroll has been my moth-eaten but still sturdy and warm bearskin coat, that when worn hangs to mid-calf and a roll of Mr. Goodyear's tent material that sheds water, big enough I can wrap in it. Alex provides us with a tarp of good canvas, enough to wrap Sarah in, and I roll two of the Hudson Bay blankets in it. Unless it turns terrible cold, she'll be fine until we reach my cabin deep in the woods.

But our leaving isn't soon enough. Before I can fork Rusty, I look ahead, and a quarter mile in front of us two riders top a small rise. If I can see them, they likely can see us.

Sarah stays quiet on Roan a few feet off the road but I, luckily, am behind Alex's wagon, so there is a chance I remain unseen. I pull one of the LeMats from its saddle holster and stick it in my belt, grab the double barrel, dismount and tie Rusty to the rear of the buckboard staying out of sight of the oncoming riders as best I can and scramble into the back of

Alex's wagon.

"Wait," he says. "I told you, I'll not go against lawmen if it comes to that."

"It won't. But if it does, I'll testify I had you under the gun. Slip your sidearm under the seat so it appears you've been disarmed. Could be these are just passersby."

Then I turn to Sarah, who seems only slightly under the influence of the demon sap. "Sarah. You sit quiet, you understand."

She shrugs.

I stay silent in the back of Alex's wagon as the two riders approach, when only fifty feet from Alex's mules, I realize one of the men is Dougle, the other I've never seen but he's a dandy in black leather waistcoat and a pair of nickel plated pistols on his hip. His wide brimmed white hat shades his face.

Sarah realizes it's Dougle and shouts out. "Will... Will, did you bring any smoke?"

Alex stands on the floorboard of his wagon and holds his hands out to the side so they can clearly see he's not carrying. His holster is plainly empty.

They gig their animals forward and Dougle shouts as they come even with Alex's mules. "Where the Hell is that worthless sogger who clubbed me?"

I stand in the rear of the wagon, unseen until I swing out with the double in hand.

"Right here, Mr. Dougle. I'm the fella with two

ounces of cut-up square nails about to blow your gut out onto the road."

The second rider reaches for a sidearm and I swing the muzzles to him before he can snatch it. "Square nails ain't picky about who they gut," I snap, and he wraps both hands around his saddle horn.

I leap down as Sarah, her voice a little on the panicky sides squeals again, "Will, you got any smoke?"

He's about to go nuts and I can see he desperately wants to draw on me, but if you've ever had the two eyes of a double barrel coach gun staring you down, you know why he doesn't reach. At this range they'd likely be holed from topknot to toe.

Rather he yells back at Sarah. "Goddamn you woman, you ain't never getting another pinch of sap from me. I hope you shake your teeth out getting off the crap. Never, never, never ever again. Where's my five dollars?"

My tone is less than tolerant when I demand, "You two climb down and keep those animals quiet."

"I'm Rollie O'Bannon," the stranger snaps. "I'd suggest you place that coach gun on the ground and give yourself up, Mr. McBain."

"If you know of me you know I have no back up in me and you've got to the count of three to dismount." With one hand I bring the double barrel up eye level and sight down it to the big man's middle. I've palmed my Colt and now have a firearm in each hand, the shotgun leveled on the fella calling himself O'Bannon, the Colt cocked and on Dougle, who's so red in the face and puffed up I'm worrying he might blow apart.

To the credit of O'Bannon's self-preservation, he quickly dismounts, as does Dougle.

"You first, O'Bannon. You two finger those shiny pistols out and let them drop."

He does so.

"Now walk ten long paces off to the side there," I motion with the barrels, "and plop your butt down in the grass, legs straight out." And he does that.

So, I can focus on Dougle. "Now you." And he drops his pistol and stomps over beside O'Bannon and plops down, but then he shouts, so mad he's blowing spittle.

"You son-of-a-bitch, I'm gonna run you down and paint the road with the blood of both of you. No man takes my woman and no woman of mine runs off."

I can't help but give him a tight grin. "Mr. Dougle, I'd suggest you find yourself another woman and get her on the opium so she can stand you. Now, both of you, pull off your boots."

"Ain't gonna happen," O'Bannon says, losing his temper for the first time.

So, with one barrel I blow a foot-round privy hole in the ground not two feet from him, and both he and Dougle scramble backwards a few feet.

"Off with the boots. Or the next one blows the legs off and I'd guess they go with them." And this time they comply.

I glance at Sarah and she's dumbfounded. I guess a little surprised that the purveyor of her sap has turned on her.

"Throw them over," I say, and both fling their boots at me. I pick them up and drop them in the buckboard, then turn my attention to Alex.

"Now, you, drummer. You get on down the road before I splatter you all over that fancy wagon."

Alex, who's been standing watching this whole thing seems relieved to not see a badge on the chest of either newcomer. He nods at me, takes a seat and whips up his mules, dragging the wagon, now with the buckboard behind.

I turn back to O'Bannon and Dougle. "You two keep your butts plastered to the grass." I walk over to the revolvers now in the grass, pick them up one at a time, and fling each one in a different direction, far as I can toss off into the underbrush, and address the men again. "I ain't no thief, no matter what seems the common notion. Wouldn't do to have you two give some grizzly indigestion so I'll leave you some defenses, if you can find them."

I move to their mounts, strip the bridles off, then the saddles and blankets, and slap them each on the rump. As they trot off, I fire a couple of rounds from the LeMats, and they gallop out of sight into the woods.

"You no good son-of-a-bitch," rings out from one of the two in the grass, but they don't try to rise.

Then I move over and strip the bridle off Roan, hang it on his saddle horn, take his lead rope in hand, and mount up.

"Just stay seated, gentlemen," I say. "We're gonna sit tight here until that wagon gets plumb outta sight. That son-of-a-bitch might come back to help y'all."

I'm covering for Alex best I can.

We don't make a move, casually letting the horse's heads down to nibble, until Alex crests the rise, a quarter mile away then wait another few minutes.

Then it's time to depart. But not before I offer some advice. "Gentlemen, I'd suggest neither of you dog my trail as I'm gonna lay up where I can do the ambush on you as I figure if you follow you've got harm on your mind. Don't get on your feet until I'm out of sight, cause if you do I'm gonna see if I'm still a fair sharpshooter with this Winchester."

Neither of them says a word. They just continue to glare at me, so I rein off leading Sarah, her remaining sap, pipe, and little firebox in her saddlebags. The coach gun now in the saddle scabbard on Roan, her mount.

As we reach the crest in the road where we'll be shortly out of sight, I look back and get a laugh as both them are limping around, among rocks and sticks, trying to find their side-arms.

If they do stay on the hunt, it'll be awhile before they can take it up again.

I imagine I've dissuaded them somewhat with the sharpshooter crack, but the truth of it is, I'm headed for the high country and not stopping until it's too damn dark to see the trail.

But, the fact is, I've heard of this O'Bannon, and of what I've heard I don't expect him to fight shy of staying on my trail like a dog on a bone.

Chapter Eighteen

The Pollock brothers, have ridden hard until they've reached the little Jackson trading post on the southeast rim of the Big Hole.

The Steinberg family has allowed them to overnight in the barn, and for a pair of dimes fed them breakfast. Gertrude Steinberg does not offer them bacon, to the brother's chagrin, but three eggs each, a pile of fried potatoes, and all the biscuits and jam they can eat.

She's also changed the dressing on Arlo's back and applied some healing salve to the wound. Were she not a chunk of lard, he'd have taken a shine to her.

The Steinberg's two teenage sons, Rahim and Benjamin, quickly finish breakfast and are sent out to harvest meadow grass as most the Big Hole is belly-deep-to-a-horse with green only now going golden.

The front of the Steinberg ranch house is a twenty-by-twenty-foot square room full of goods, as nicely arranged and as good a selection, for a small store, as the Pollocks have ever seen.

Adolf Steinberg is a big man with a generous middle, but Jethro, in studying him, thinks there's very little fat involved. He guesses the middle-aged farmer is strong as an ox and is glad he's sent his equally large sons off to work, as he doesn't want to deal with all of them. Mrs. Steinberg is as round as Adolf, but a foot and a half shorter and likely more suet than muscle, her graying hair pulled into a bun and covered with a dust cap.

"We'd be lookin' to buy some goods from y'all," Jethro says, standing from the table and motioning toward the trading post portion of the building.

"Ya," Adolf says, and pushes his bulk away from the table.

He's insisted the pair leave their weapons out in the barn before entering the kitchen to take their breakfast, so Arlo heads for the kitchen door and mumbles, "Got to saddle up."

He has both their horses saddled and waiting at the hitching rail in front of the store before his brother is through with his shopping. He dismounts, carrying both his Winchester and his brother's Sharps into the little post.

He is just in time.

Steinberg is behind the counter, Jethro across from him. A cloth sack the size of a nail keg rests between them, more than half full of goods.

"Show my brother the '73'," Jethro says, and Steinberg hands the shiny new rifle over.

"Damn," Arlo says, then expels a low whistle. "If that ain't pretty as a brindle topped New Orleans whore."

Steinberg is obviously offended but says nothing as he senses the men want the new fifteen dollar rifle. If so, it would be the most expensive firearm Steinberg has ever sold.

"How much?" Arlo asks.

"They come very proud," Steinberg says.

"How proud is very proud?" Jethro asks, recovering his Sharps from his brother, and checking the load, which obviously makes Steinberg nervous.

"Well," he stammers, "Winchester insists we sell them for the full fifteen dollars retail. But since you boys had breakfast and paid good money for mama's cooking, I'd let you have it and a box of .44 rimfires, fifty to the box, for only that fifteen dollars. Plus two dollars and seventy-nine cents for the supplies, of course."

"By God, I'll take her," Arlo said, and Steinberg smiles widely. But his smile fades when Arlo swings his Model 66 to center on the big man's belly.

"You don't understand," Arlo grins widely, "I said I'll take her, not pay for her."

"But...but," Steinberg stammers again.

"No buts about it, Kaiser William," Arlo says, sarcastically, then turns to his brother. "Go make sure the missus Kaiser don't have a scatter gun nearby, and bring her here. Then take a gander out the door and make sure those two dumb whelps of their'un ain't coming back this way."

"We got law, hereabouts," Steinberg says, his jaw setting hard.

Arlo laughs as Jethro strides out into the kitchen, where Mrs. Steinberg is cleaning up. Then he says, in a low growl, "We done set the Bannack City law to chasing their tails out toward the sunrise. You just stand quiet while Jethro fetches your woman."

"What are you gonna do?" Steinberg says, his voice low, as Arlo shoves his wife into the room.

"Just making sure the both of you is mindin' your manners. Put your head on the counter there, Kaiser," Arlo said.

"Why dat?" Steinberg says.

"So you don't see us leave. Don't want y'all to know which way we go."

"Dat make no sense," Adolf says.

"Just do it so I don't have to shot a hole in that big gut of yours."

Mrs. Steinberg speaks up for the first time. "You go to Hell you shoot some innocent."

"Beelzebub wouldn't have me, lady. You go around behind the counter and you put your noggin alongside ol' Adolf's, so you can't see no how neither."

Adamantly, she stomps around, and Arlo motions with the muzzle. Adolf does as he insists, and she follows his example.

With a full swing of his rifle, Arlo smashes Adolf's head and blood flies, but Mrs. Steinberg reacts by shoving away from the counter and comes up with a little belly gun they must have kept beneath the planks.

She's not fast enough, as Jethro has his Sharps leveled on them and the blast of the big .45/.70 rocks the place. The slug takes Mrs. Steinberg between her ample breasts and she's blown back into the shelves of goods behind. Several cans clatter to the floor as Adolf slumps there and she falls across him.

"Grab up them vittles," Arlo instructs his brother, "while I find a few boxes of cartridges for my new rifle."

"Your new rifle?" Jethro complains.

"Yep, to bad they ain't two of them or you'd have one too. Hustle your ass a'fore we gotta waste more shells on them dumb whelps."

In moments, they're mounted and loping off down the two track. As Arlo glances out into the field, he sees the boys abandon their thrasher and run toward the trading post.

He waves at them, and laughs as they ride on.

***

Sheriff Sean O'Leary and five townspeople from Bannack City camped thirty miles northeast of town on the Beaverhead River. As they'd packed up that first morning they ran into the third party on the road between Bannack City and Virginia City, and they, like the others, had seen nothing of the Pollock brothers on the road.

O'Leary turns to the others after chatting with the last passersby, "Gol darn it, boys. I think we've been hornswoggled by those two owlhoots. Let's head back and see if we can see where they left the trail."

It's dark when the limp into Bannack City and go their separate ways. O'Leary, a single man, is able to get to Matia's Good Eats just as he's locking up.

"Matia, how about loadin' me up a pie tin before you hightail it. I'm beat to a frazzle from trying to ride down those two bandits."

"No luck? I'm not surprised. Hoy was in today and said they come by his place and one of his doves patched one of them up. Seems you sliced a grove in the older ones back. They rode out toward the Big Hole."

Sean sighs deeply. "Too bad it wasn't through his ugly noggin. Give me a plate full if you'd be so kind. Come in early and I'll have all the boys here just before daybreak for breakfast—if any of them will keep up the chase."

In moments Sean has a plate full of cold food

and heads to Mattie's Boarding House, where he has a room. He's decided to fill his gut. As much as he hates to stay awake, he makes the rounds of the others to see who's willing to ride on with him for the dollar a day and found the city's paying for dangerous posse work.

He won't blame them if none of them keep up the chase.

Chapter Nineteen

Acting Sheriff and owner of Holland's Sean O'Leary is surprised when Percy McDonald, the barber; Arnholt Richardson, a hostler at R and R livery; and Gustave VonStadt, all agree to ride on at dawn. Doc Henderson, who has a couple of failing patients is the only one who chooses to stay. And Sean is glad he does as one of the patients is his brother, Vernon.

Sean's up before the sun, even though his butt aches and his back screams at him. He's normally in Holland's little kitchen or doing a shift behind the bar. Horsebacking and filling in for the Sheriff is not a normal thing, but he's not one to shirk his duty.

The four of them ride out as the sun clears the mountains to the east, stop for only a short time at Hoy's to verify what Sean had been told, then charge on at a lope.

It's early afternoon before they see the Jackson Trading Post in the distance, and are surprised to see the two hefty but young sons of Adolph Steinberg driving a cross in at the head of a mounded grave on a hillside just behind the buildings. As they near they see another grave dug and a body in another pine box next to it.

"What happened here?" Sean asks as he reins up.

"Two no-goods robbed pa and ma and shot them down."

"We are riding after two who robbed my place, Holland's, in town." Then he turns to the others. "Let's give these two a hand," he yells, and they all dismount.

As they work, the older of the two boys pauses a minute and turns to Sean. "I doubt you remember us, Mr. O'Leary. I am Rahim and that is my brother Benjamin. We will close up and ride with you, as soon as we read over ma and pa."

"How old are you?" Sean asks.

"I am eighteen and Ben is sixteen."

"You might do but your brother is too young—"

"We will ride with you or we will ride alone. But we will seek justice for ma and pa no matter."

Sean shrugs, nods, then asks, "You got good animals and weapons? If we catch up there will be some shooting."

"I would hope so," Rahim says, then returns to shoveling the last few shovelfuls onto his mother's grave.

He and his brother both wash up in a large pewter pitcher they've brought to this little cemetery—now begun with two graves—then read from the Torah, and recite, "May His great name be blessed forever, and to all eternity." Then to Sean's surprise, both rip their shirts over their heart.

Then, still with torn garments, head down to the barn and soon have a pair of large mules saddled and a third one packed with large panniers.

Both boys reappear wearing sidearms and have Winchesters in scabbards on their saddles.

"One thing," Sean says as the boys rein up beside him. "You two are to stay at the rear of this thing. I don't want to be responsible for burying the last of the Steinberg's."

Both boys remain silent, giving only a small nod in return, and Sean hopes they've taken to heart his instructi—but doubts it.

They again set off at a lope across the Big Hole.

***

The same time the Bannack City posse leaves the Jackson Trading Post and Tag McBain and his sister find their way to the Salmon/St. Mary's wagon road, four hard men are riding south out of St. Mary's Mission in the Bitterroot Valley. Each man drags a spare horse, lightly packed, which they alternated riding. They've been on the trail for a week, riding east along the Mullin Road, then south through the fifty-mile long north-south valley.

Just as Seth Rheinhart hired Rollie O'Bannon and the Pollock brothers, General Theodore McTrippen, owner of the GTM Silver Mine in Silver Valley, brought the Delgado brothers and their associates, Sanford Schultz and Porky Adler all the way up from Sacramento to ride down the woman who'd stabbed his son to death—a woman with scarred hands, a whore, who went by Sally Macintosh at the time. He subsequently learned she also was known as Sally Maddox and of late as Sarah Dougle.

The four men he'd hired were the most trail-tough and ruthless he could find, and he'd offered them one thousand dollars each should they bring the woman back to him, alive, so he could hang her from the fir tree that grew only forty feet from the front door of his office.

Mark was his only son. A son he knew was reckless, a wastrel, and had a mean streak—but still an only son.

Humberto 'Bert' Delgado, the older of the brothers, is leader of the pack. Tall and thin, pockmarked from a bout of smallpox, given to smoking short cheroots, he's given up the sombrero he'd worn when the brothers and their cohorts fled Los Angeles, on the run from the law for stealing horses, and rode through the swampy San Joaquin Valley to Sacramento. He and his brother now both sport flat brimmed hats usually attributed to the Spanish. In Sacramento they saw General McTrippen's notice pasted on the post office bulletin board, and immediately wired him with their qualifications which they embellished. But the boasts worked and they received a draft for one hundred dollars expense money and headed out for Idaho Territory, figuring it was far enough from Los Angeles they'd be insulated from Southern California wanted posters. They brought cohorts with them to make a posse of four.

The Delgados are half Yaqui Indian. The Yaquis are renowned for their tracking ability and their dogged pursuit through some of the most inhospitable county in North America, the Sonoran Desert. Sanford Schultz is a quiet man of average size and sports a Cavalry hat he'd worn through most the war, until he deserted. He has a reputation for carrying a short blade in his boot and using it with the slightest excuse—and any slight is an excuse. Porky Adler has a belly the size of a nail keg but otherwise is on the spindly side. It's his pig eyes, nearly yellow in color, that likely earned him the handle Porky, in addition to the watermelon he carries as belly. Even so, he's been known to ride fifty miles a day without complaint, so long as there is a fine—or even foul—smelling woman and bottle at the end of his trail.

All four are hard-as-the-hubs-of-Hell trail-tough, rattlesnake-mean, and have ridden both from and for the law across most of the Southwest.

When only twenty miles south of St. Mary's Mission, they pull up as they come face to face with a pair of big black mules in front of a large freight wagon towing a buckboard. A strange contraption this far out of any town of size.

They rein up off the road and await the oncoming wagon. As he nears, they notice he places a revolver on the seat beside him and a Winchester across his legs.

"Howdy," Bert Delgado says, in a friendly tone, and gives the wagon a tight smile and small wave.

Alex pulls rein on the mules and they stop.

Bert continues, "That's quite a train you got going there."

"It is that. How far on to St. Mary's Mission, since y'all are coming from that way?"

"Ten or twelve miles. Where'd you come from?"

"Last real stop was Bannack City. Headed to St. Mary's to peddle some farm implements."

"Yep, read your sign. Passed a few farms twixt here and there, if you care."

"I care," Alex says. "Where y'all headed?"

"We're on the hunt for a woman. She stabbed a young fella dead over Silver Valley way."

"Don't see any badges on you fellas."

"Private lawmen, hired by the family. Don't imagine you run across a woman name of Sally, or maybe Sarah?"

Chapter Twenty

Alex could feel his face flush, and he tries to shake his head but he twitches nervously and says nothing.

"Damn if you didn't," Bert says with a small guffaw. "And just where did you see this Sally or Sarah? You stop and partake of a soiled dove by that name?"

While Alex is talking to the dark-skinned thin man, who sucks on a small cigar after every sentence, the other three gather around the wagon one on the side of the man talking, the other two take up positions opposite. Then one of them dismounts, a pot-bellied fellow with small yellow eyes.

Alex clears his throat and manages to say, "You got that all wrong, stranger. I haven't seen a woman since Bannack City, and only a half-dozen there. Rare as hen's teeth, it seems."

The man who had remained horseback opposite the speaker also dismounts. The first one has climbed up on the back of Alex's wagon, investigating the contents. The one who just dismounted takes up a position alongside Alex's mules and puts a hand on the halter of the gee-side mule, Alex guesses to make sure he doesn't whip them up.

As soon as he has a hand on the halter, the man doing the talking dismounts and moves over to Alex and points to the ground.

"Get your ass down," Bert snarls.

"Why?" Alex replies, but the big man reaches up and grabs Alex's upper arm and drags him off the wagon and throws him to the ground. Then steps on his windpipe.

"Now, I'm gonna ask you again. You see this woman?" He reaches in his shirt pocket and pulls out a folded paper and spreads it and holds it so Alex can see. "This here woman, name of Sally or Sarah or God knows what now. Easy to identify as she got her paws in a fire and scarred up and is never without gloves."

Alex, flat on his back, has both hands on the man's ankle of the foot on his throat, trying to keep him from shoving his heel to the back of his neck. But the man eases the pressure and Alex manages to motion with a shrug, then grabs the ankle again.

"I guess I'll just have to put my weight on this here foot until your skinny neck snaps."

Alex tries to speak but can't. He shakes his head best he can.

So Bert asks, "You wanna tell me something?"

Alex nods, the best he can.

Bert takes the weight off enough that Alex can speak. "Let...let...me up," he coughs and rubs his throat before continuing, "and...and I'll tell you."

The man pulls a long Arkansas toothpick, a foot long blade sharpened on both sides, from his belt, and places the point on Alex's Adam's apple. "You tell me a lie and you'll be picking your tongue up outta the dirt."

"She's on the trail with her brother," he admitted.

"What trail, where?"

"This trail, back a day's ride or so, last I saw."

"Going or coming."

"Passed me back near the Big Hole. Coming this way."

"We ain't passed them here."

Alex shrugs, hoping the point of the blade doesn't pierce his throat.

Bert shoves the blade deep enough to draw blood. "You don't know where they was headin'?"

"No idea. Just passed them on the road."

"Then how'd you know they was brother and sister?" The knife is about to break skin.

"We chatted, like some passersby might do."

"What's the brother's name?"

"Hunter. That's all he said. No last name. Please, the knife."

Bert did ease it up a little. "You got any vittles in that there wagon?"

"Hardtack and jerky, and a bit of left over haunch of antelope."

"Here's a quarter," Bert stands and digs in his pocket and drops a quarter on Alex's chest, "so dig out what you got, hand it over, and we'll get along."

Alex hurries up on his wagon seat, digs in the back, and hands Bert the foot long antelope haunch, only half the meat gone, and a small sack full of hardtack and venison jerky. He says nothing.

"You can buy or trade for more in St. Mary's," Bert says, stuffs his saddlebags full of his purchase, and whips up his horse.

Three of them lope off but before Porky does, he cackles, then yells, "You a lucky, pilgrim. I'm real surprised he didn't roast you in that wagon." Cackling again, he whipped up his mount and followed.

They slow to a quick walk and Bert turns to his brother. "We ain't passed them so they either camped up or turned at that fork the sutler told us about. Down toward Salmon City. Get your tracking nose on, Ortiz, and we'll have a pocket fulla' gold coming before the week's out."

***

We've stopped twice plodding down the very steep road since turning south at the divide and crest of the Salmon City-St. Mary's road, for Sarah to fire up her little glass globe and suck on the smoke from the sap. There's some real chill in the air which makes me want to push it as we're three days to my old cabin, and I'll need time to ready things for winter, including filling the smokehouse and woodshed.

I don't complain about stopping as we need to blow the horses and even more so as I know she's about out of sap. Thank God. I say that with some trepidation as I know life will soon be pure Hell as she tries to get body and soul back to normal, I worry that the cravings may never stop. If not, her life is ruination.

By the end of the day we've descended at least two thousand feet in elevation and it's warmed a tad. We've crossed a small creek several times and it's now large enough to be home to a few fish. In my gear I have a few feet of line and a half dozen small hooks. I put Sarah to clearing us a spot under a large fir and find myself a few tiny beetles for bait, In only minutes have a dozen six inchers. Carving a little fat off the chunk of hog belly, and with the application of my steel and flint, I soon have them frying. It's my habit to keep a small canteen in addition to my sweet water and it most always has a couple of handfuls of red beans soaking. With a little salt and some wild onions I've pulled from streamside, we have a feast.

After supper, as I clean my little frypan and pot, she smokes the very last of her sap.

Come morning we'll find out how strong my sis is.

Chapter Twenty-One

The Pollock brothers see a man on horseback and one afoot as they ride at a canter to the west on the two track.

After McBain and the woman had ridden on, Rollie O'Bannon quickly found his well-trained black, got saddled and mounted, then soon located his revolvers. However, he was bootless and he wanted to resolve that issue before pressing on.

Will Dougle, on the other hand, was not so lucky and was still afoot, although he too found his sidearm.

So, they were plodding back to the Jackson Trading Post, Rollie horsebacking, Will limping along in front, with saddle and bridle slung over his shoulder. Rollie didn't trust him enough to have him at his back, particularly when the man was desperately in need of a mount.

When only halfway back to the post, in the grasslands of the Big Hole, they are surprised to come face-to-face with the Pollock brothers.

"By all that's holy," Rollie says, "you two made it all the way to Bannack and pressed on."

"We did," Arlo replies. "Where the Hell is your boots, Rollie?"

Rollie's face reddens then he mutters, "Got dry-gulched by McBain. He was hiding in some drummer's wagon with a scattergun. Soon as I get shod again I'll be back on the trail and skin that son-of-a-bitch when I catch him."

Arlo and Jethro both laugh, and Rollie reddens even more.

"Ain't a damn bit funny," Rollie mutters again, then his voice hardens. "He's riding with a woman and they likely can't move fast." He points at his companion. "Dougle here was shacking up with the woman and we have reason to believe her to be McBain's sister and there's posters out on her. Y'all ride on. Soon as I'm shod—likely they got something at the Jackson Trading Post, if not in Bannack—I'll hotfoot it after you. Now get on with it."

Rollie can't help but notice that Arlo is sporting a brand new '73' Winchester in his scabbard, but it's not the time to visit about armaments.

The Pollock brothers are still smiling as they whip up their horses and ride on, only reining up when out of sight.

Arlo waves his brother up alongside him. "You think they can lay that bloody mess at the trading post on us?"

"Hell," Jethro says, "them farm boys know it was us, so it's likely the whole world will know soon enough. We shoulda ventilated their hides as well."

"Let's get this McBain and his woman cold and across a saddle and then worry about how to get the reward collected."

They whip up their mounts and move on at a lope.

Rollie is growing impatient at having to plod along with Dougle limping ahead. "Dougle, I'm gonna ride on. I'll try and bring you back a mount if you got the money to pay."

"The Hell you say," Dougle sputters. "If you was half a man you'd trade off me riding."

"I'm a man and a half and one who didn't let his horse run off. You got the price of a nag?"

"I got plenty of poker winnings. But it's pure chicken shit you leaving me."

"I'll be back with a mount and it'll save you walking."

"Go on, you som'bitch. You better come back or I'll live to piss on your grave."

"Bold talk for a man limpin' along twenty miles from nowhere."

"Just come back quick."

Rollie only gets a couple of miles down the two track when he reins up as a half dozen riders are pounding his way.

They rein up and before he can question them. The man in the lead snaps, "I'm Sean O'Leary, acting Sheriff of Bannack. We're tracking a couple of louts who robbed…" he hesitates to admit it was his establishment… "who robbed a saloon and then murdered man and wife and robbed the Jackson Trading Post. You see two riders passing?" Then O'Leary glances down. "Don't oft times see a fella riding in his stocking feet. Where the Hell is your footwear?"

"Long story." He hopes his reddened face doesn't give away his embarrassment. "What about these two murderers?"

"Ugly ill-kept louts, one wounded with a bullet crease across his back from my weapon. Likely a bloody shirt. The larger of the two is mounted on a palomino and the smaller a hammer-head dappled gray. They pilfered some firearms from the post."

Rollie is not eager to lose his associates, as rotten as he knows them to be, to a posse. At least not before he captures McBain, but he knows Dougle is limping along behind and will surely tell all he knows.

"Passed a couple of fellows a few miles up the road, but didn't stop to visit and have no idea what they were riding. I'm being followed by a man of foot, who you may know as he was a recent resident of Bannack—"

"On foot? Who might that be?"

"Dougle, he said. Big fella, big as me. He was

riding with me when we had some trouble. I'm riding on to replace my boots and gather up a horse for Dougle."

One of the posse riders spurs his animal forward. "Jackson Trading Post belongs to my brother and me. There's four riding horses in the corral and tack in the barn. Help yourself and leave the critters on your return at the post or in Bannack."

"That'll be Dougle's responsibility. I'll be following after y'all as soon as I'm properly shod."

"Footwear in the post. Boots are three dollars the pair. Leave the money on the counter you find something suits you."

"I won't be picky," Rollie says.

The Sheriff touches his hat brim, "We're riding on. If you go on into Bannack report the murders at the post and that we're riding on."

"By the way," Rollie asks, "any reward for them you're hunting?"

"Not yet, but we don't catch them the city will likely pony up one."

Rollie gives them a nod, and they spur up their mounts and gallop past.

***

Bert Delgado waves his brother, Concho, up alongside as they lope along south. "We should be at this

Lost Trail pass come sundown, then we gotta figured which way to go. They came outta Bannack the drummer said, so if we don't come on them I'd guess they turned south, maybe headed for Boise City."

"Near full moon tonight," Concho said. "We could ride on over the pass till we find water, if you're of a mind to."

"Let's hope they turned this way and that'll solve our problem."

Chapter Twenty-Two

I figure we're two, maybe three, days to the Salmon Trading Post, where I can likely buy a pair of pack horses or mules and stock up enough dry goods to last us most the winter. There will be meat a plenty—fish in the creek, grouse you can kill with a rock, and deer, elk, and maybe a bear for a real winter coat for Sarah as fine as mine. I don't know what I'll do if my old cabin up in the Selway has been claimed by others and can only hope not. Or if so, it's someone I can eject with a clear conscience.

And I hope Tennessee Tom Maxwell still is the proprietor of the Salmon Post, and for that matter, that the post is still there. If not, we'll have to stay low and head on south. There will be no taking a woman into the high-country winter without proper supplies and cold weather gear.

Sarah is visibly shaking as we saddle up, and she eyes me with some contempt as I'm sure, in her condition, I'm to blame for all that ails her. After all, I've taken her away from her supply of sap.

As I suspect, when she mounts, I get an ultimatum. "I have to go back now."

"Sarah, it's three-day's-ride back to Bannack, for a good rider who's well. We got to press on." It's lie time again. "It's less than two days to my cabin, where you'll have all the sap you can smoke for a year." Fact is, it's at least a week to my cabin.

"Tag, I know there's plenty back at Hoy's, I don't know what you say is true."

"Have I ever lied to you, Sarah?"

"When we were children, yes, I'm sure you did."

I can't help but smile, then it's serious time again. "Well, little sister, we ain't children no more. You're gonna ride with me away from all that ails you, and we're gonna get you as pure as when we was children. And that's the way it is."

She's mounted. I've yet to mount, but have a hand on her horse's headstall. She tries to jerk her animal around, but I have a tight grip. The scattergun is in her scabbard on the far side and she reaches to drag it out, so having no choice, I jerk her out of the saddle, throw her on her butt, and Roan shies away a few feet. The scattergun is flung aside.

I'm not gentle, with her flat on her back, and I put a muddy boot between her breasts. "Know that what I do is because I care for you. You'll never put that poison in your lungs again, so long as I live. Now, we can ride on, or we can wait out your body getting clean? Your choice. How some ever should we wait you'll likely hang over in Idaho as we're likely being pursued."

She's wide-eyed, but it only shows me how unhealthy she's become. The whites of her eyes have a yellow tint. She sputters, "Tag, it will kill me. I've been on the smoke for half a year. I can't—"

"You can, and you will, and you'll do it in short order as there are folks on our trail who'll put a hemp rope around your neck and mine if we don't keep moving. I'll give you one full day, then it's ride on if I have to tie you in the saddle."

"I'll likely die," she says, softly.

"You'll likely wish you were dead before this is over, but you'll live to laugh again."

"Fetch my bedroll and build the fire back up. I'm dizzy and know it'll be worse."

So, I do. I get her settled then lead Roan and Rusty across the little creek to a small meadow and stake them out of the sight of the road, with their tack near at hand. Then as I return, collect as much dry wood as I can carry. I won't do to have smoke roiling above the tree line.

Now, God willing, those on our trail have headed toward the Bitterroot, or have given up.

But that's likely a fool's dream or supposition.

We're set up a good fifty yards off the road, not a dozen paces from a stream I could nearly leap across, under the thick boughs of a fir. I use the boughs for tent rafters and a the tarp traded from Alex for a tent. I build a tiny fire to warm the space and caution her not to build it higher. The thick fir will disperse the smoke, but I worry the smell might be noticeable.

When all's arranged, I caution her. "I'm going away back up the trail. I've left you the canteen and some hardtack and jerky, can you stomach it?"

"Can't," she mumbles.

"Like I say, I'm going back up the road. I'm taking Roan so don't have any thoughts of riding back to Bannack."

"Why are you going back?"

"To check our back trail. From a spot I noticed back a ways I can see the road for more than a couple of miles behind. We need to know if we're being dogged."

"Leave me a weapon."

"Not yet. You might be tempted to use it on yourself, or more likely me. Lay there, keep warm, I won't be long.

I only drag Roan behind me for a couple of hundred yards, then take him down near the creek and stake him out in some deep grass.

Now, it's see who might be following.

***

The Pollock brothers reined off the trail a few miles short of Lost Trail Pass, found themselves a flat spot by the stream that fell their way from the mountaintop, and camped for the night.

Arlo's back was healing, at least not bleeding, and he was able to rest as Jethro broke out some jerky and hardtack, and a can of peaches he'd stolen from the Jackson Trading Post.

No more than ten miles behind the Pollock brothers, Sean O'Leary and his posse, along with Rahim and Ben Steinberg, made a late camp along the same creek.

Well past the east branch of the Bitterroot River, and only a few miles short of Lost Trail pass, Bert and Concho Delgado, Sanford Schultz and Porky Adler make a dry camp and enjoy the antelope haunch they've 'bought' from Alex Engstrom.

And Alex Engstrom is camped near St. Mary's mission and has walked on to the rectory, where lights appear in the windows.

He's been sick at heart since telling the four foul men about Hunter Talbot—he wonders if that's a real name—and his sister and has decided he must try and make amends. It's his plan to leave his wagons in the care of the mission, for which he'll offer a generous tithe and to take two of his horses and enough supplies for a few days, and ride back—changing horses time-to-time so not having to rest them—and see if he can pass the four men and catch up with Hunter and Sarah and warn them.

He feels as if he's a coward, and it's torn at him since he parted ways with the four head hunters, who he surmises will shoot down both Hunter and Sarah without so much as the slightest warning.

For some reason, Alex took a liking to poor Sarah, who seemed so overwhelmed by the smoke to which she was obviously addicted. He sensed that under her pain and the ravages of the evil smoke she is a beautiful woman, should she be rested and well and her eyes not as hollow as worm holes. There is a sweetness about her, even in her besotted state. His own mother had been addicted, but not to opium, rather to English gin, but it, too, was an abomination.

Before sunup, he'd backtrack and see if he could redeem the evil he'd done the brother and sister.

Chapter Twenty-Three

I perch on a rise not far off the road and watch our back trail until nearly dark. Then I head back when figuring I'll get back just as it is too dark to see.

Gathering up Roan I lead both horses the two hundred yards back to where I turn off to find the big fir, unsaddle and stake the horses out again, then poke my head into our little makeshift shelter.

Only to discover my sister missing.

Damn, damn, damn.

I back out and yell for her. "Sarah! Sarah! Where the Hell are you?"

I get no answer, then hear retching coming from the direction of the stream, and hurry there. It's so dark I almost trip over her, on her hands and knees, dry heaving.

Helping her to her feet I let her lean on me until I get her settled among her blankets. She's immediately in fetal position, her hands on her belly, alternating between low moans and louder retching.

It's going to be a long night.

Before I try and get some sleep, I finish off the hardtack and jerky I'd left her, which has remained untouched.

Placing a couple of pieces of jerky in the pot in two inches of water, I hope they'll soften overnight and provide Sarah some soup when she wakes, should she be of a mind.

I awake long before dawn, stoke up the little fire and seeing her with eyes open caution her again, "I'm going back away to watch our backtrail. I'll refill your canteen and leave you some hardtack. Set the pot on the fire as it's got a smidgen of soup you might be able to stomach. You'll need the sustenance. I'm taking the horses."

She nods but looks as if it takes the last of her energy to do so, then again folds into a fetal position and moans.

Again I leave the roan only a couple of hundred yards away and water him before I stake him out.

I've replaced both LeMats in their saddle holsters and have the Winchester in its scabbard. What I'd give for a Sharps as I can see the road for a good long way. I know without doubt we're being tracked. I have no interest in shooting down some townsfolk doing their civic duty; not so disenchanted about shooting some bounty hunter who'll likely come at us for the money, and not care if it's bringing us in dead or alive. I would have no trouble blowing the backbone out of the lout who calls himself Will Dougle, who got my sister a slave to the demon smoke. In fact, she's confided some of the horrors he put her through, and I've a mind to hunt him down even if he's not dogging our trail. But I'll worry about that at a later time.

Now it's time to get her somewhere she can heal up, and we can both avoid the thirteen turns of a hemp rope. As soon as I'm confident we're not about to be overtaken.

The rise I've chosen from which to watch our back trail is a little over a half mile from our little camp and looks down on a mile of wide meadow before the road climbs again. Even then, I can see some edges through and above the trees as the road climbs back toward Lookout Pass. I'd guess I can see, in spots, as far as two miles.

The meadow, which is edged by the little creek on its east side, is flanked by pine and fir-covered slopes and tangles of brush, thick in spots and thinner in others.

Doing the recon on the country is an old military habit. As a captain in the cavalry it oft times meant life or death for not only my mount and myself, but for my company which ranged between a hundred and three hundred men. So, it was an imperative habit to develop and one not dulled by time.

It's cold in the pre-dawn, near freezing or maybe

a few degrees below.

And clear.

A good day for a fight, if there's ever a good day.

So, as the line of sunlight creeps down the slope to the west, I take up a position on a rocky edge, and wait.

***

Alex Engstrom had not been able to sleep and finally arose and saddled his big black when the moon was still high in the sky, and dawn, he figured, hours away.

He put the black into a comfortable lope, dragging the bay behind—a gait he knew the animals could keep up for more hours than he'd be comfortable in the saddle.

It was nearly three hours later, with the sun just lighting the eastern mountain tops, when he reined the animal back, then moved him down to a trickle of water and let him rest. Lather dripped from their withers and flanks, but they recovered quickly.

He was only a little surprised when the black traded neighs with another animal that couldn't be more than two or three hundred yards away.

Alex got back in the saddle and eased his way back to the road then kept a sharp eye down the slope as they moved on at a comfortable walk.

As suspected, he saw a camp a little over a hundred yards below the road, a camp still at rest except for one man stirring the fire. He watched the man carefully as he passed, and the man didn't look up, nor, luckily did the black trade neighs with any of the eight horses tied to a picket line.

When he was two hundred yards beyond the camp, which he was sure were the four men who'd accosted him on the road, he gigged the black into a lope again. After a mile he had to slow to a brisk walk, even though the road was now well lit by the quickly rising sun. His arm and back ached from dragging one horse while he rode the other. He gave the lead rope as much slack as he could and tied it off to his saddle horn. That was fine so long as the trailing horse kept up. When he slowed the lead cut into his thigh.

Rollie O'Bannon had no trouble finding the trading post or the horses stabled there. He even found a pair of boots that fit his size thirteen feet. As the sun was already behind the mountains to the west of the Big Hole, he decided to stoke up the fire in the Steinberg's house, fix himself a stew from a side of beef hanging in the settler's smokehouse and help himself to a quarter of an apple pie he located in the pie safe.

Will Dougle would make do on the trail, which served the sogger right for losing his horse.

At sun up, well rested, Rollie finished off the stew, picked himself the best of the four horses, a straw-berry roan, and another, a piebald for Dougle, tied his string lead-rope to tail for the two he dragged, and covered no more than a mile before he came upon Dougle straggling along.

"I don't imagine you brung me some vittles," Dougle said, without bothering with a good morning.

"I don't imagine. You shoulda told me what size boots you wear and I would have brought you a pair."

"I'll take the strawberry," Dougle said, and reached for that lead rope.

"He's my backup. You'll take the piebald."

"Humph," Dougle managed, but didn't argue as his feet were so sore he'd have cried out if you touched them with a powder puff.

As he was saddling, Rollie instructed him, "The trading post is only a couple of miles. There's a pot of coffee going cold on the potbelly, a half a pie in the safe, and more than a dozen pairs of boots. Get there, get fed, get shod and get your ass back on the trail. I'll be alternating a walk and a lope. You keep up a lope and you'll catch up before high noon. If not, I'll wait an hour at the forks. You understand?"

"I'll be along," Dougle said and mounted up and loped away without looking back.

"You will or you'll not make a damn dime, and you will make an enemy no man can survive."

O'Bannon turned back to the task at hand catching up with the Pollock brothers, then riding McBain to ground.

Today could be the day. Then he could head back to Nemesis, collect his money, and with luck in a fortnight he'd have his feet in front of the fire at the Brown Palace Hotel in Denver.

Chapter Twenty-Four

Sitting peaceful, watching our back-trail, gives me plenty of pause to think on this past year.

Before that, I was as content as a man can be carrying the load of years of trying to kill my fellow man who I had no grudge against—only Mr. Lincoln's word it needed doing—and coming away from that with blood on my hands and soaked deep into my soul. It has dried there and a part of me has gone rancid. Then after years healing in the high country with only me, my dog, my horse, and a couple of mules for company, I had a shock that no man should receive, hearing my sis and her family all murdered at the hand of a heartless cattle king over a lousy squirt of water. Then, after another month of blood and wrath—working vengeance for her and hers—the shock of discovering her to be alive, or at least possibly so.

Again the blood bubbled up hot and refused to cool until I found her, alive, thank God.

But still, even though she in fact remained alive,

the death of six scum-suckin' pigs was earned by them for the murder of her husband and two daughters. A fine man and tiny angels so beautiful the sight of them, the one time I saw them, would bring a man to tears.

And did, when I learned of their death.

And all that revenge, as it's turned out, for the sake of a woman who's been working hard trying to kill herself with demon sap. A woman who might not live through the night or may take her own life with either the pain or the shame of it.

Life plays strange tricks on us, as if God's an imp trickster, who spends his days laughing at our trials and tribulations.

And, I fear, the killing isn't over. It's likely us or them and "them" might be some needin' killing or some honest townsfolks thinking they do their civic duty, and "us" being killers rather than the avenging angels we likely fancy ourselves.

Finally, my observation is not in vain. And, as it's early afternoon, I'm just about to go back and check on Sarah. It's a good thing I became lost in my thoughts.

A single rider, coming at a lope. I spot him high up on the mountain—maybe two miles from me—a movement the size of a gnat, only visible as he rounds a steep ridge above the tree line.

I don't see him again until he's less than a mile

away, coming onto the flat. He's coming like a man with a purpose dragging a second mount. Loping in the tougher steeper pieces of road; actually galloping in the flats.

Setting up with the Winchester in a dark shaded cleft of rocks, I pick a spot with a clearing through the trees only seventy-five yards from my muzzle. There's only two men who might be pursuing us who I'll recognize. Both big men, damn nigh half again my size. One of whom I've seen only one time.

I'd hate like Hell to kill the wrong man, to bend over his body and discover it's not Will Dougle or the man who rode up to Alex's wagon while I hunkered in the back. Rollie, I believe he said, and he wanted to arrest me so I presume him to be a bounty hunter. If so, a fancy one, in black leather waistcoat and nickel-plated revolvers.

If this is either of those two, they recovered quickly from my relieving them of boots and horses.

Of course it might not be Will Dougle or this Rollie fella, and still be someone who wants my hide or head to sell for the bounty.

As the rider nears, he's in and out of sight as trees preclude my getting a decent look at him. So, I settle down, calm my breathing as a sharpshooter is trained to do, and await his appearance in the clearing only seventy-five paces away.

I cock the Winchester, sight carefully, rest my finger on the trigger without pressure...then jump to my feet and uncock the rifle as I run, crashing through the underbrush, to intercept the rider.

"Alex!" I yell, as my newfound and only friend of late almost gallops past.

He reins the big black gelding—lathered from chest to withers—to a sliding stop and leaps from the saddle with more athleticism that I would have guessed. He pulls his wide-brimmed hat off and beats the dust from his trousers, all the while looking at me and talking rapidly.

"I've had a Hell of a night and day. I rode out in the middle of the night, worried I'd offered you and your sister up to some devils. Four men passed me on the trail yesterday afternoon—hard men—asking about who I presume is your sister. I saw a poster on the trail, describing what could be her." He looks questioningly, but I don't respond so he continues. "Those four looked like stone-cold killers to me."

I merely nod, and he rattles on.

Then I passed four more and had to ride off the trail as I recognized them...at least two of them—those two who braced us yesterday."

"How far behind?" I asked.

"Some miles, I'd imagine. They were moving at a walk—a determined walk—but a walk."

That gets me moving. "I got to fetch my horse."

"Wait," he snaps, and continues. "I don't want to

be responsible—"

"Alex, I've got to get my horse."

"Where's Sarah?" he asks.

He's ridden hard to warn us and I can't imagine he has harm in mind, so I tell him. "She's back down the trail, a half mile or so."

"Let's get her and get the Hell away."

But I have another thought. "Alex, if you're willing, you get her. That roan she was riding is only a hundred yards, maybe two hundred, this way from our camp, staked out near the creek. Get her in the saddle, and ride on. I'll catch up and meet you at the Salmon Trading Post. Should be a day or day and a half on down the trail."

He's chewing a knuckle. Then quits and asks. "Is she okay?"

"No, but I hope she's good enough to ride. But you make her ride, which will be a chore. But it's likely ride or hang. I'm gonna to slow these boys down."

"Can you keep me out of it?" he asks.

"I have so far and will do everything I can. But you've got to move if you're willing to help."

He strips the saddle from the black and saddles the bay, mounts that horse and glances back at me. "Try and not get yourself killed."

"Just gonna make 'em move more carefully and that will slow 'em down. Way down."

He gives heels to the game black, dragging the

well lathered bay, and gallops away.

I fetch Rusty, give him heels, and gallop back to where I see another rock pile surrounded by a thick stand of lodge pole pine. I rein off the trail, move around behind the rock pile and tie Rusty fifty paces deeper into the copse.

Then I hotfoot it back to the rocks and set up where I can see back up the road a quarter of a mile and have some view of the road climbing away up the mountain.

Making sure the Winchester is fully loaded and checking the loads in my LeMats, I settle in.

I don't have to wait long. I see the dust before I get a glance of the riders—four of them—a half mile up the road.

They're coming hard now.

Chapter Twenty-Five

I steady my breathing, glad there's only four of them and that the other four Alex talked about haven't joined up with them. But they came to make time. Each horse they ride carries only a small set of saddlebags and reach rider drags a second mount—it too only burdened with a small pack.

Then I swallow hard. Not more than a quarter or three eights of a mile behind them, up the mountain aways, come five more riders. They, too, are pounding trail and raising a dust cloud.

I might have been able to scatter four of them into the brush, but nine?

I consider jumping on Rusty and riding hard. Then I have another thought.

They aren't riding together. Are they at odds? Or do they even yet know there are two groups of highbinders vying to trade our hides for a pile of greenbacks or cold gold double eagles?

From the pile of rocks I can quickly disappear into the lodgepole behind, and if I've judged the country can cross the creek and move through the trees on the hillside opposite the creek and back to the camp. Maybe I'll be able to catch up with Alex and Sarah.

At least escape my hideout in the rock pile without being seen.

Now, to test my theory about these two groups of bounty hunters not being allied.

I sink lower into the rocks when the first four come into view—maybe three-eighths of a mile across the flat. They're moving at an easy lope. About the time they come even with me, the other four appear.

Letting the first four pass I wait until the second group are maybe two hundred yards up the road and the first four two hundred past, then take a deep breath.

I'm more than a fair shot, having done some sharpshooting during the war, and with my first shot at some one hundred and fifty yards, the lead horse of the following bunch stumbles, then goes down.

Moving a little way back into the trees, I can see the first four rein up and scramble off the road into the rocks and trees hunting cover. Just to add insult to injury, I bang one off the rocks near where the leading for had scrambled.

The second four are likewise scattering as one of them rides up and loads the now afoot rider whose horse tumbled after my shot, onto the back of his animal, and kicks up dust barreling into the trees.

So, I figure it's time and lob another shot at the first group. To my great satisfaction gunshots and gun smoke fill the air from their direction.

But not at me.

And the second group fills the air with gun smoke and the canyon echoes with gunshots.

As I watch they spread out and two from the first group move at a trot back toward the second. The groups are too far apart—well over three hundred yards—for their volleys to cause much damage, but I can only hope.

I can't help but laugh.

I've started a war and this is one I can leave behind without suffering so much as a crease on my hide.

With the canyon roaring with gunfire, I hustle back through the trees to Rusty and we pound across the creek and up the heavily timbered slope until we turn south.

I can't gallop or even lope, due to the thick cover, until I'm a half mile down the canyon; then turn back and cross the creek and pick up the two track road.

Pausing for a moment to let Rusty blow, I break out into a true guffaw, even slapping a thigh. The occasional gunshot still echoes down the canyon.

Whistling *When Johnny Comes Marching Home Again*, I move south on the road at a comfortable lope, then slow to a single foot.

I've only gone maybe four miles when I see Alex

and Sarah up ahead. All three horses are loaded with our gear; Alex leading Sarah and Roan, with the bay trailing not fast but determined. Sarah is slouched forward, head sagging, almost on Roan's neck, obviously still sick as a poisoned pup.

I rein up beside Alex and he almost leaps off his horse, so startled.

"I figured," he says, "you were shot full of enough holes to mimic a sieve. Sounded like Gettysburg back there."

"Not a scratch." I say with a wide smile. "Seems those two groups of hooligans did not appreciate the competition from each other. I seriously doubt we will again have as many on the hunt as you saw this morning. Should any of those louts be decent shots."

"Well, sir, what I saw they deserved each other. I'm pretty sure there won't be a crowd of mourners singing *The Old Rugged Cross* over their grave, if anyone bothers to bury their rotten carcasses."

***

When O'Bannon, Dougle, and the Pollock brothers reached the saddle on the road out of the Big Hole where it tied to the Salmon-St. Mary's road, they had a decision to make. Did McBain and the woman head north to St. Mary's or south to Salmon? They decided to try north for a while, hoping to run into travelers who might have seen them pass.

After five miles, they decided it was enough… besides, all the track they saw was headed south, and unless McBain had stayed off the road, they should have seen at least two animals headed their way.

They reversed their course, and were surprised to discover, after reaching the saddle again, that their track out of the Big Hole was totally obliterated. Maybe a dozen horses, shod horses, had passed, and turned south.

What the Hell was that all about?

As they rode along, Arlo Pollock motioned for his brother to fall back. When they had sixty feet or so between them and O'Bannon and Dougle, Arlo nudged up close to his brother. "Lots of damn horses. You suppose that posse turned and come our way?"

"Hell, who knows. No matter, they be ahead of us and we'll likely see them long before they know we're doggin' 'em."

"That makes some sense, Jethro. My back is achin' me something fierce. Dig that pint outta your bags."

"Done drunk it down."

"I hope it turns to vinegar and pickles your damn gut."

"Let's catch up." Jethro gigged his horse into a trot.

Chapter Twenty-Six

Acting Sheriff Sean O'Leary had just spotted the four riders some three or four hundred yards ahead of them on the road. As they seemed to not know of the posse's presence, he was shocked when he heard the report of a rifle, and his horse collapsed under him.

O'Leary had been a clerk during the recent war and had never been shot at. He fell hard, landing on his face, knocking the wind from his chest and leaving him gasping for a moment. When he did get to his feet and heard the report of several more rifle shots and the buzz of lead nearby, he figured he'd better get to cover. He'd only taken a couple of steps when his leg gave no support and he fell again.

Arnholt Richardson, the hostler, had heard the buzz of many a mini-ball and spurred his horse, leapt from the saddle and got O'Leary on his feet. He mounted, then gave O'Leary an arm and swung him up behind. Without more blood being spilled, they reached the trees and were out of sight of whoever was ahead firing at them.

Fire was quickly returned. Arnholdt and Percy

from near the road, and others from higher on the hill.

Arnholdt quickly removed his belt, and almost before O'Leary realized he'd been wounded, bound his upper thigh and quelled most the bleeding.

To his credit, O'Leary sat back up and as his other posse members were not in sight, yelled, "Gustave! Percy! You boys okay?"

Percy's voice came back. "Gustave took one through the side. I'm stuffing the wound with what I tore from my shirttail."

O'Leary yelled again. "Steinberg's, where are you?"

Arlo's voice rang down the hill from slightly above them. "We're good—up the hill aways in good cover.

"Stay down," O'Leary said and crawled back near the road. To his surprise, looking back up the road for his boys, he saw another four riders on the road coming their way.

"What the Hell?" O'Leary managed.

"What?" Arnholdt questioned.

"More riders. They got us wedged in. Gimme that bandana."

Arnholdt wondered what the Sheriff wanted with his neckerchief, then was surprised when the Sheriff tied it to his gun barrel and began waving it. It wasn't white, but he presumed the Sheriff was surrendering.

To whom, Arnholdt had no idea, but he was.

Over three hundred yards in front of those who'd shot at him, Bert Delgado was spitting mad. Not that he'd been shot at, but that his brother was on the ground pumping blood from a through-and-through wound from scapula to just below the collar bone. He dragged him off the road and into the cover of some jagged granite.

"Son of a bitch," Concho Delgado spat, stuffing a chunk of neckerchief into the front side of the wound where the slug had blown a chunk of flesh more than an inch-and-a-half wide.

Bert yelled at his other bounty hunters. "San, you and Porky okay? I want you to go up the hill and flank these drygulchin' bastards."

"Porky won't be going. He's got a hole in his fat guy with suet stickin' out."

"Then you go." Bert pulled a railroad pocket watch and glanced at the time. "It's 11:25. I'll give you fifteen minutes to get in position."

Sanford's voice came back, "Damn if they ain't waving a flag. You suppose they want to surrender."

"Who gives a shit? They shot Concho and Porky and we're gonna leave them for the buzzards. You understand...*comprende*?"

"I got it. Twenty to twelve I'll be above them."

Bert turned to his brother. "I'm gonna go get a few

hundred pounds of flesh for that couple ounces they took from you. You rest easy. We'll be back."

Rollie O'Bannon had pulled rein when the commotion began down the mountain and sat studying the situation when he saw the flag begin to wave.

"Now, what the Hell do you suppose that's all about?" he asked Dougle who was next to him. The Pollock brothers were fifty feet behind.

Arlo Pollock turned to his brother. "Jethro, you don't imagine that damn posse turned around and got ahead of us?"

"No idee, but if so, seems they're givin' up."

"They go to tellin' O'Bannon what we done did and he likely won't take it favorably."

"Let's play it out and see what comes, Arlo. Whatever it is, we can handle it."

O'Bannon turned back to them. "You two keep back a bit. If things go bad watch who your shootin'. Let's move on up."

O'Bannon, with Dougle at his side, closed the hundred yards between him and the man with the flag at a trot. When forty yards, he realized it was the Sheriff from Bannack, and he relaxed a bit.

He reined up near O'Leary. "Sounded like a war up here," he said.

O'Leary nodded. "Don't really know. A gang up ahead just lay down on us."

Then O'Leary looked beyond O'Bannon and stared. Was that the two thieves who'd robbed him?

The Pollock brothers had slowed to a walk, but kept coming until only twenty feet behind O'Bannon.

O'Leary looked over his should to see where his fellow posse members were and was not comforted as he saw no one. Gustave nor Percy were to be seen. Had they lit out? He turned back nervously. O'Bannon sat his horse with a hand resting on one of his nickel pistols, Dougle next to him, gazing around as if he thought his woman was somewhere in the weeds. And the thieves....

As he glared at the two dirty men behind, he was shocked to see them both blown out of the saddles, hitting the ground hard.

O'Bannon's horse shied to the side, tangling with Dougle, but he got it under control and was pulling one of his Colts when two more shots rang out behind O'Leary and blood spurted from two fresh holes in O'Bannon's black vest. He spun his equally black mount and gave spurs to the animal, but slipped from the saddle before he made fifty feet.

"I ain't part of this," Dougle yelled, his hands raised, but he, too, gave heels to his mount and with his hands still in the air, it spun and galloped back the way they'd come.

Things had happened so fast O'Leary had no time to even get his chin off his chest. He glanced up the mountain to see the Steinberg boys, both with rifles raised, reins tied around saddle horns, their horses picking their way down the mountain. The he turned and looked over his shoulder he saw Arnholdt and Percy coming forward at a trot, carrying their Winchesters.

Arnholdt got there first and, wide eyed, asked, "Sean...Sheriff I mean...that fella was drawing on you, weren't he?"

Chapter Twenty-Seven

Percy was close behind and he sputtered, "I guess both of us thought so as we both shot."

Then O'Leary looked back to see the Steinberg boys arrive, both with rifles still trained on the Pollocks.

Rahim glanced over as they neared. "Those two are dead, right, Sheriff?"

O'Leary answered, stammering a little, "Haven't had time to check."

The instant he got it out, both boys aimed and fired again, and both Pollock bodies jerked.

"Damn, damn, that's enough!" O'Leary yelled.

Rahim looked over. "The Hell—wish I could kill them again, only slower."

"Scabbard those Winchesters. That's enough."

Seeming satisfied, both boys slipped their Winchesters in saddle scabbards.

"Help me down," O'Leary commanded Arnholdt and Percy, who dragged him out of the saddle and got him settled on his one good leg. He stood like a stork, his shot leg folded up, using his Winchester for a cane.

The boys both swung their horses and Arnholdt announced, "Got to get back to Jackson. We got stock to feed and hay to put up before the snow flies."

"Why, why, hay…" O'Leary yelled after them. "We gotta bury these three."

Arnholdt yelled back over his shoulder. "Bury that one y'all shot if you want. Them two will make a fine pile of coyote shit. Stop by on your way back and we'll stand you to some vittles." With that, Arnholdt adjusted his wide-brimmed hat and they gigged their horses away.

Bert Delgado arrived on the mountain on the far side from where the Steinbergs had made their stand and settled into a pile of rocks a hundred yards up the mountain. As he'd made his way through the thick pines and firs, he'd heard several more shots. Were the damn fools shooting down the road where he had left his brother and Porky? He hoped those two had the good sense to stay low.

Sanford Shultz, also wondering what the shots were all about was on the far side, near where the Steinberg's had been. He glanced at his pocket watch. One minute and he should hear Bert fire and he could begin picking off the…. He glanced down. Three men. Three on the ground. What the Hell?

They'd only seen five. Had there been another, and had their return volley of shots killed three of them outright? Or had the damn fools got into it between themselves? He was a little flummoxed. But what the Hell. Whatever had happened, the odds were better. Now two ag'in' three.

He zeroed in on one man, then realized the man was using his Winchester for a cane. Hell, he was wounded. Switching his aim to one of the others, he waited for Bert's signaling shot...but it didn't come. He studied the other side of the canyon and made out Bert working his way closer, moving from tree to rock pile to tree.

San adjusted his cavalry hat so his eyes were shaded and watched as the two able-bodied men started dragging two of the dead ones off the road, then came back and hoisted a big fellow, belly down, over the saddle of a horse which had wandered back down the road. The two men doing the work had leaned their Winchesters on a rock while they worked, and the wounded man was using his for a cane.

As San watched Bert grow closer, he decided the bossman was either getting close enough so he couldn't miss, or was going to take the three prisoners and let his wounded brother have his way with them.

Sanford actually got a chill down his back, thinking what was in for those three should Concho and

Porky—if Porky was still alive and mobile—be able to torture the three as they'd talked about torturing others. After all, Huberto and Concho were half Ya-qui. They knew torture.

While one of the men, obviously the wounded one, leaned on his Winchester and held the horse now loaded with the body of the big man in the black vest, the others stripped away gun belts and weapons and began piling rocks on the bodies of those they elected not to haul back to town. The two filthy men already stank, God knows how they might smell in a few days.

As they worked, Bert Delgado stepped out of the willows lining the little creek, rifle in hand and sweeping back and forth from man to man.

"Belay that. Let them rot where they lay," he said, then clamped his jaw and glowered at the three who remained alive.

Arnholdt brushed his hands off on his pants and glowered back at the dark-skinned stranger. "Now, just who the Hell are you?"

"Unbuckle your gun belts and let them drop," Bert snapped.

"I'm the Sheriff..." O'Leary tried to say, but was interrupted.

"I don't give a rat's ass if you're Jesus J. Christ. Drop your gun belt and let that Winchester fall or I'll kill you where you stand."

O'Leary glanced over and saw another man step out of the trees just up the hill.

"And who the Hell are you…you two? These men were wanted in Bannack for theft and committed murder over in Jackson."

"You have one more breath to take, you don't drop your rifle and gun belt," Delgado growled, then stepped closer to Percy and Arnholdt, who were complying.

Sanford came out of the trees and walked up behind O'Leary, who had yet to unbuckle his belt and crashed his rifle butt across the side of O'Leary's head, and he went down in a heap. San grabbed up his revolver and Winchester.

"That wasn't called for!" Percy yelled, taking step Sanford's way.

And it gained him a smashing blow from Bert Delgado's rifle, and he, too, fell in the road.

"What's the meaning—" Arnholdt cried out. Then to his surprise two more shots rang out and the man who'd clubbed O'Leary dropped his weapon and O'Leary's and his arms wind-milled as he took three steps back then fell unmoving.

Bert Delgado spun away, dropping his rifle, went to his stomach and began dragging himself toward the creek, blood blossoming on the back of his shirt.

Arnholdt looked around, confused, then grabbed his rifle up to be on the ready for whatever came, but he was the only man left standing.

Hoof beats rang out and both Steinberg boys appeared, horses trotting their way.

"Who were those bandits?" Rahim, the oldest asked. "Least I hope they were bandits."

"Reckon they were," Arnholdt managed. "They clubbed the Sheriff and Percy down."

"That one's still kickin'," Benjamin Steinberg said, motioning at Bert Delgado who had made the stream and was trying to keep his head out of the water.

"Leave him be," Arnholdt commanded. "Enough blood today to last a lifetime." Then he turned to the boys. "What brought y'all back? Not that I'm not glad you returned."

Rahim nodded. "Seems we're glad as well. Benjamin left his hat up the mountain. Pa bought him that hat and ma made the woven hatband for him. It's a particular good keepsake, under the circumstance. You gonna be okay here? We need to tend to the home place."

"Hell no I ain't gonna be okay. I got three dead men here and at least two unaccounted for. There was four up ahead of us and only two here."

Rahim sighed deeply. "We'll hang until we get them two planted and we know you don't face trouble from more of them."

"Obliged," Arnholdt said, and glanced over at

Delgado whose face was now in the stream and he was unmoving. "Looks like we got another to bury. Wish we had a shovel."

"Rocks a plenty in the stream." He dismounted, but turned to his brother Benjamin. "You keep watch for them others while this hostler and I go to work. Looks like the Sheriff is coming around, and Percy is stirring some, so maybe we'll have some help.

Chapter Twenty-Eight

I figure it's no more than fifty miles from the crest of the pass to Salmon and we made at least a dozen when we'd camped and where Alex joined up with us.

So it's another nearly thirty miles to Tennessee Tom Maxwell's Salmon Trading Post, and I pray he is still in residence and running the tiny outpost. He and I were fine friends, the half-dozen times I was down out of the high country, trading firs for necessaries. He's a fair man and at the moment I could use a friend.

Sarah is some better, a long way from recovered, but has stopped the dry heaving and seems able to perch in the saddle without support. I've been able to untie her legs from the latigo. Alex seems more than merely attentive. Maybe my sister's needs and the fact that somewhere beneath her worn and sickly exterior she's a beautiful woman has brought him back—that or the fact he felt he was feeding us to the wolves when he confessed our whereabouts to that bevy of bounty hunters.

I still have to chuckle at starting a war between those two groups who were on my tail and hope that, if any of them were honest citizens they escaped unscathed. But by the number of shots I heard as we made our escape, I'd be surprised if none were not at least wounded.

We make camp where the creek has widened to a dozen paces across, under the cover of thick firs. Sarah is able to take a cup of jerky soup broth and keeps it down, so I'm mightily encouraged.

Alex takes a spot near the fire, leaning against the thick trunk of a fir, and Sarah's head nods until she lays it down, to my slight surprise in Alex's lap. He gives me a somewhat embarrassed smile, but doesn't move and rubs her shoulders until she's deeply asleep.

I know he has a business, a trade to take care of, and wonder how long he plans to accompany us?

It will be interesting to see.

I'm a little surprised when he speaks to me before I fall asleep. I plan to rise early and backtrack to make sure we're not being pursued too closely, so I've closed my eyes with the sundown.

"What's your name?" he asks. "Your real name, although I think I know, Mr. McBain."

I sit up and wrap my arms around bended knees. "You've surmised correctly. And like all wanted men,

I'll tell you—and it's the God's honest-truth—I'm innocent of murder. Guilty as Hell of killing a passel of men, but not guilty of murder. All of them slayed in self-defense or in defense of family or friends."

"And Sarah?"

"What little I know she was forced to the soiled dove business to survive…not much caring if she lived or died after her husband and two daughters were murdered by the very scums I'm accused of murdering. Anyway, a…a, shall we say, customer... threatened her with a knife and she turned the tables on him and he wore his own knife between the ribs. The Hell of it was, his daddy was a powerful man, and a vindictive one, likely bought the law and put posters out on her. So, here we are."

"I'll be truthful. I see something in her, something good and pure. She's like a puppy that's been mistreated. In her case, mistreated by life. I truly hope her life is better from now on."

"If I have anything to say about it, it will be."

He chews on that a moment, then asks, "You ever been to California?"

I eye him carefully for a moment. "Thought of, after the war, there or Oregon, but only made it as far as the Selway. But I barely got two nickels to rub together and it's a Hell of a long hike."

"Let's get all these bounty hunters and law dogs— if that's what they are—well behind us and talk on it more. You're an affable sort and I'd guess you'd do fine selling implements."

"Never thought about it, but I guess a fellow could do worse." The fact is I've thought of it often. I left a lady, a lady named Lizzy, who, although a lady with a past, was a supporter of mine at a time I was holed in thigh and side and damn sure in need of a friend. And only hours before the culmination of a prior month or more of Hell's fire and gun smoke she became much more than merely a friend. A lady's goose-down bed is not a bad place as hideout. And it was her suggestion we meet up in San Francisco and go into the saloon business, a trade she is somewhat an expert at operating. The fact is even more obvious to me, I'd like to pass a lot of time with the lady, no matter her success.

I hope her offer stands.

O'Leary has a quandary.

He is wounded and needs to get back to Bannack and the doctor, but he has men to bury and one he's sure should be hauled back. Just O'Bannon's fancy accouterments, and of course his notoriety in Leslie's Weekly, says there might be someone out there who'd like to see him have a decent burial.

And he has at least two others somewhere out in front of them who they should hunt down. After all, they'd shot at a duly constituted posse only doing their job.

He called the Steinbergs, Arnholdt, and Percy together with the hope of a consensus, and got one. Rahim, Arnholdt, and Percy will remain behind to try and build cairns over the bodies from river rock—after all, they have no shovels—and to mark the graves with willow branch crosses. Young Benjamin will ride back to Bannack, leading the horse carrying O'Bannon, make sure they got there safely, care for his stock at the Jackson Trading Post, then return with shovels in case they need to trim up the graves decently.

To Hell with the other two men who are out ahead of them, and to Hell with McBain and his sister. They can ride on to Hell as far as O'Leary is concerned. He, after all, is only a substitute Sheriff. When the real Sheriff returns maybe he'll want to ride out after McBain, but the fact is McBain did nothing to offend Bannack, and the two filthy men who had were soon to be under a layer of stone that only a grizzly could dig up.

Now, if only his leg wound didn't go green before he could get it cared for.

Dougle had caught O'Bannon's fine black horse, which he figured to be a stud, and led him at a canter heading back to Bannack. He figured to sell the animal and it's carved and silver-trimmed saddle and bridle, and keep going to Virginia City or maybe Helena. He had no idea how many men were bleeding out on the ground at that mess back on the Salmon road and could care less. He was whole, had a fifty dollar or more horse and at least that much in saddle and bridle, if he found the right buyer, and that would get him a new start in someplace distant. When he got to the Big Hole he slowed to a walk. He didn't want to kill the black stud, not that he truly thought he could run such a magnificent animal to death, and he was sucking as much wind as the animals.

If he didn't get enough for horse and tack in Bannack, he'd lead the stud onto Virginia City, then if not there, to Helena. Both were full of miners with pockets full of gold, and he'd likely get even more.

When fellas got their pockets full of gold, their brains seemed to shrink along with pockets filling.

Me, my sister Sarah, and Alex Engstrom rode straight through to Salmon. Since the last time I'd been to the post the spot had grown. We passed a couple of decent farms on the flats before reaching the post, and a half-dozen cabins and one decent house surrounded the place.

I was more than a little pleased to see Tennessee Tom Maxwell behind the plank counter of the expanded trading post, now added on at the back with Tom's residence grown much larger. I soon saw why, as a plump blond girl with a German or Norwegian accent walked out of the back and called out, "Welcome," as we entered.

Tom looked up, grinned widely, then turned serious and looked around with some worry in his eyes.

"Tom, how the devil are you?" I asked as the big burly man rounded the counter. He smiled wide again and extended a hand.

I shook with heartfelt enthusiasm, as Tom turned serious again.

"You've had some trouble since riding out. What's it been, two years?"

"Almost. And trouble still dogs my trail so we won't be staying long."

Tom turned to Alex. "Didn't you sell me some iron implements a couple of years ago?"

"Guilty," Alex said. "But this isn't a sales call."

Then Tom asked, smiling at Sarah, "And who might this be?"

"My sister," I said, but didn't bother mentioning her name. "She's a little under the weather."

Tom waved the blond girl over. "Ingrid, you've heard me speak of Tag McBain. He's here in the flesh." Then he turned back to Tag. "My wife, Ingrid."

"Well, sir, congratulations."

"Ingrid," Tom said, "please take Tag's sister back and fix her a cup of tea and give her a piece of that wonderful apple pie you made this morning."

The women left the room and Tom watched them go, then turned to Alex and me. "You can't stay here long. There're posters all over heck and gone on you and your sister. And we have a Federal Marshal and judge due here anytime, escorted by a squad of troopers. Maybe even this afternoon."

Chapter Twenty-Nine

"You're having a trial here in this little berg?" I ask.

"Dang if we ain't. Some ol' boy on down the river went a little crazy this winter and killed his wife and four children. Wasn't discovered until summer was over and they was dried out like some of the salmon we hang after pulling from the river. A terrible thing."

"You can make a jury here in Salmon?" Alex asks.

"We can, but it'll take every man from twenty miles around."

I slap the big man on the shoulder. "Guess we'll be cutting our visit short. Couldn't stay long nonetheless as some others may be dogging our trail. Tom, I got about fifty dollars—"

Alex interrupts. "Tom, you give us whatever Tag needs. I'll back him up."

I give Alex a tight smile. "I guess you're coming along with us?"

"Got to make sure Sarah is gonna be fine," he says, and colors a little.

"You're welcome to ride with us until you tire of us," I say.

"Not likely," Alex replies, and glances at the door Sarah left through. "I made a deal with the priest back at the mission. He's to sell my goods and wagons and I'll wire him where to send my share."

I believe Alex is a bit smitten.

I eye him a minute. "Alex, Sarah and I don't need much, particularly if my place is vacant." Then I turn Tom. "You hear anything about folks taking up in my old cabin on up the river?"

"Don't know, Tag. We have a dozen or more fellas come down from the mountains, trading hides and jerky and fresh meat from time to time. But none have mentioned coming all the way down from the high country and finding a ready-made cabin."

"How about a boat?" Alex asks.

"A boat?" I question before Tom can answer.

"Yep, a boat." Tom says. "This river goes all the way to the Snake, and from the Snake it's not far to the Columbia, and then it's an easy float to Port-land—downstream all the way."

I hadn't thought of floating out, but know there's probably not a breathing soul between this post and the Snake River, and likely not a poster between from there to Portland. Tom is proving to be more than merely a fine drummer.

I turn to Tom. "Anybody do that, Tom?"

"Saw a few fellows leave here floating that way. Don't know of any who made it, but haven't heard of any who didn't make it. I do know there's some rough water that way. The river of no return, it's been called, so it's damn sure a one-way trip. But, yes, I've got a pole boat, shallow draft, with a mast and sail that I will sell."

I laugh. "Thought this was a trading post."

"Sure as heck is," Tom says, returning my laugh with a wide grin.

So I begin the dickering. "We've got four fine horses—"

"Not near as fine as my boat," Tom says quickly, the trader coming out in him.

So I add, "And a few extra firearms. But we'll need the best part of a month's grub—grub that water won't ruin. A few implements and some duds that'll fit Sarah."

"You got any coffee brewed?" I ask, then turn to Alex. "I've banged head bones with Tom many times. He's a tough but fair trader. Let's drink his coffee until he folds."

"It's not me that's pressed for time," Tom gives us a canny smile, then adds. "I imagine that federal judge will be accompanied by a troop of cavalry, and that Marshal will have posters memorized."

"Then let's get to the end of it. Four horses, four firearms, including my two LeMats. And you throw in grub for a month, a hatchet, and some duds for a serviceable boat."

"Ha, why don't I just give you the post as part of the deal? That, and a hundred dollars in gold and you have a deal."

We dicker for another ten minutes and I throw in twenty-five dollars as does Alex. Then we head down to the water's edge to inspect this craft we will trust with our lives.

As we walk out, Tom grabs a jug of whiskey off the shelf. "I throw this in. Hate to have one of you get snake bit with no medicine at hand." He laughs loud enough to shake the dust out of the rafters.

Tom is a fair hand with adz and plane and as I suspected the boat is sound. A five-foot beam, twenty feet long, two fine lockers as water tight as one can make them lined with Mr. Goodyear's rubber cloth, their seams watertight with tree sap.

She's a double ender with two sets of oars and a shallow rudder operated with attached tiller, which should work out fine if Sarah is soon well enough to perch aft and keep us in the middle of the flow. Missing the many rocks in this wide shallow run before we get into the canyon a few miles downstream will be a chore—I presume the river deepens as the sides narrow.

The nearly five-foot-wide and eighteen-inch-deep lockers are under two hinged seats, each seat with gunnel oarlocks on either side. Tom even has provided a pair of spare oars. Near the trading post the river runs wide and shallow this late in the year. The boat, even with the three of us and our month of stores, only draws eighteen inches of water—thank God as we'd likely scrape bottom if her draft was any deeper.

Tom only knows the waters five miles or so downstream from the post, near where the river enters the narrowing canyon—going on would mean commitment all the way to the Snake—and has had no reports from anyone who ventured farther. And farther is into the canyon that earned the stream the moniker 'The River of No Return.'

Hell, there could be a hundred-foot waterfall between here and the Snake. That would sure as Hell result in 'no return'.

However—nothing ventured, nothing gained. As soon as we're packed with foodstuffs, bedrolls, firearms, tarps for tents in which we wrap spare clothes and bedding, and some fishing gear, we say our goodbyes and set out.

I've become attached to Rusty, my gray with the unusual rust spots and, as part of our trade, make Tom swear to either keep him or only trade him to a kind and competent soul. He's been a fine friend and faithful mount.

As Sarah and Alex take a seat, with Tom and me

left to push us off, she snaps at me as it dawns on her, "You lied to me. You have no poppies."

I ignore her and change the subject. "And how was Ingrid's pie?"

"Humph," is all she manages.

Obviously, even as sick as she's been, Sarah is still desperate for the sap. I'm sure it will be a week or more before those dull sunken eyes return to the beautiful flashing ones I remember.

"Let's go," I say, ignoring her. Tom and I push off and I get wet up to my thighs before I clamber over the gunnels. I wave to Tom.

It appears we've left just in time, as in the distant approaching the post are a half-dozen troopers and a couple of fellas in a buckboard.

The twelve foot mast is stowed, the sail wrapped around it. Alex is on the forward oars and I move Sarah to the middle seat, leaving those oars folded, and take up the tiller.

Yelling to Alex, I suggest, "Stow one oar and use one to fend off."

She responds to the tiller but not as quick as I'd like. The water as far as I can see is fairly flat, with only white water where a rock parts the stream. So far it's easy going. Sarah grabs a blanket and sinks off the seat and to the bottom and rolls up like a cocoon. I'm pleased she does as if the water gets rough—and I know it will—I won't have to worry about her going overboard.

We must be making six or eight knots and I'm managing to stay clear of the rocks, Alex only having to bear off on one so far—and it almost threw him overboard. It will be a learning process.

"You want to take the tiller?" I yell at him.

"Let's make it until it's time to find a flat to camp on. I'll take it tomorrow!"

We're on the water for a half hour, northerly, before the river suddenly bears west. The river narrows, but only a little, and still is lightly peppered with exposed rocks. It's the hidden ones I worry about.

Alex has been giving me hand signals when suspicious of hidden obstacles; we've scraped a couple but nothing so hard I worry about our thick plank hull. Two pans with handles are on three foot tethers and will be used to bail should we take on water—and I know we will. But so far it's only been a few splashes over the bow.

As the river narrows, the slopes on either side rise gently, spotted now with scrawny pines and undergrowth.

The sun to the west has disappeared behind the mountains, so I yell to Alex. "Look for a good spot!"

Chapter Thirty

It's less than five minutes when he waves me to the north shore and I'm able to swing her bow between some rocks higher than our gunnels. When we're only feet from dry land, Alex jumps with bowline in hand. He throws a bosun's hitch, and we're secured to a rock and there's a sand flat easily big enough for the three of us to spread out.

He and I both leap out and push the boat higher on the bank, but get little purchase as she's a heavy craft for only the two of us. She spends the night snug against the downstream rocks.

"I'll fetch some firewood," Alex says and starts into the near undergrowth.

"Hold on. At least take your sidearm. I'm getting used to having you around and don't want to feed your ugly hide to the critters."

He laughs, but comes back to the boat and reaches into the forward locker under his seat, straps on his revolver, then heads out.

I scoop out a shallow hollow in the sand and make

a fire ring of rocks, fetch a slab of bacon and a couple of large potatoes from our stores, wash them in the river, and slice them on a flat rock. My head snaps up when a shot rings out from no more than fifty feet away through the brush.

Even Sarah rises and looks around.

I grab my Winchester and charge into the brush toward the shot. Then after only a dozen strides up the slope, shoving through the brush, stop and smile. Another forty feet away, Alex already has his knife in hand and is opening the belly of a whitetail doe.

He turns and shouts. "She stood up not twenty feet in front of me, revolver range. Fresh meat!"

"Mr. Engstrom," I reply, "you're handy as a pocket in a shirt. You go cook some of that bacon for the grease and get some of those soaked beans to cooking. Let me finish the doe. I've skinned and butchered a hundred or more of them."

"Sounds like a deal," he says, and still smiling wipes his bloody hands in the grass and heads on by me.

In short order I have the doe gutted, skinned, quartered, and her loins and back-straps fileted out, then haul the first load the few paces back to camp.

Alex is cooking—a pot of beans on some coals he's dragged from the main fire, a skillet on with grease popping in the bottom. Sarah is perched on a nearby rock and I hear her as I approach.

"Alex, I should be doing that?" she questions with furrowed brows.

"You'll have more than enough chances before we're in Portland," he replies, with a wide grin.

She nods, then curls up on a blanket in the sand. She's still dressed in the same gloves, long skirt, flannel blouse, and wool coat she's worn since we left Bannack, and all are now filthy. I traded Alex out of a pair of wool men's trousers her size, a couple of flannel work shirts, and the smallest pair of brogans he had. First I want her to eat, then I plan to heat her some water and insist she change clothes, wash and stow the old ones, and take a sponge bath while Alex and I climb the hillside and see how far down river we can see to try and gauge what comes tomorrow.

Being clean, smelling fresh, is the first step to feeling human again.

I'm encouraged by the fact she's offered to help and even recognized that something needed doing.

I can't help but believe today has been a lark, compared to what's ahead.

Washing the quarters and loins in the river, shedding the meat of hair and blood from the process, I then wrap and stow the packages. The water in the river is cold as Hell, so I store them at the bottom of the lockers against the hull, with only the thickness of Mr. Goodyear's rubberized cloth between them and the hull and beyond the cold, cold Salmon.

With the liver in hand I return to the flat rock and slice it up. What we don't eat tonight we'll have for breakfast and lunch on the river. Tomorrow, if we finish off the liver, it'll be heart and beans or spuds.

God willing, in a week we'll be on the wide slow Snake. God willing.

Morning comes with the sky pewter gray and flat as grandma's pressing iron. And, for the first time, there's ice on the puddles near the river. I worry about what the flat sky is hiding? What we don't need is an inch of rain to set the river to bucking and roaring any more than she already is. As it is, since the Salmon Trading Post, she's now only half the width and, I'd guess, more than four times the depth.

As I close my eyes after the day's light has totally faded, I ponder about how one's path is changed by events. Alex's joining us has turned us into sailors, of sorts, and our destination is now Portland rather than San Francisco. From Portland, or before, I can wire Lizzy and see if she still has an interest in tying up with a wanted man. Some fine steam-driven ships ply the waters between Portland and San Francisco.

As has been my curse since a youth, I'm the first one awake, and lay wrapped in my bearskin coat and watch the sky begin to lighten to the east. Then I hear a shuffling and a snort in the brush—and not far from our camp.

Another habit, developed early and polished to a

shine during the war, is sleeping with my firearms in easy reach. Quietly, I pull on my boots.

I fear I know the source of the sound and blame myself, as I should never have left the gut pile so close to camp.

Picking up a few dry sprigs of grass, I test the wind, which seems to be blowing due easterly out of the canyon. The gut pile is only slightly to the east and fifty feet or so north, so odds are, if it's a bear or cougar working the pile, it won't wind me. I edge into the brush, carrying my Winchester with a .44/.40 shell seated and the hammer back.

As careful as I'm putting them down, I hear a small branch crack underfoot and freeze.

No more than thirty feet in front of me and slightly upslope, a full grown griz stands on back legs and tests the wind, almost my worst realization, until her two yearling cubs stand beside her and emulate mom's defensive action.

I should have awakened Alex; one of the many things I should have done.

The smaller bears drop out of sight, back on the gut pile I presume.

But mama stays on her hind legs, then a nose that's been sweeping back and forth stops, and I can see her bad-vision beady eyes trying to focus.

On me.

Chapter Thirty-One

Staying so still I hardly take a breath, I watch, squinting so my eyes show as little as possible. There's an eight-inch-trunk-diameter pine tree close enough that I'm partially occluded by its branches. A possible safehaven. But climbing high enough before she can get to me is out of the question, and even if I make it, Sarah and Alex are only steps beyond. I have killed many a bear, but that was with my old Sharps .45/.90 which I've left somewhere far behind. My .44/.40 Winchester will do the job, but not before she has time to tear me limb from limb. She'd likely die with a bellyache from chewing my ugly hide and taking a pill of lead or two, if I'm fast enough.

I should have taken my best head or neck shot while she stood with lots of brush between us, but she drops out of sight as does the opportunity. She's angry and I know has scented and likely seen me. She's gnashing her teeth, snapping, and growling. But not charging, yet, as I hear no brush breaking.

Taking a couple of steps back, my eyes not leaving where I think she'll break through, I'm startled by a sound behind. I cut my eyes and it's Alex, in stocking feet, his lever action in hand.

"Bear?" he whispers.

"I wish. Bears. Mama and half-grown cubs."

"Not good," he says, unnecessarily. He paces me, both backing away.

We don't get far when a roar and busting brush causes me to drop to a knee with my rifle shouldered. Alex is behind me and I hope leveling his rifle.

She does crash through on all fours, then to my surprise, when seeing us again rises on hind legs, roars and throws her head slinging spittle. My lucky shot takes her in the mouth with head back, and Alex fires almost so quickly our shots almost sound as one.

The griz manages to light back on all fours and leaps, once, then with the second is on me and sends me flying to the side.

I'm trying to recover my feet and lever in a shell at the same time, then realize she's still. Lying on Alex, but still.

But she's not the only problem. Her cubs are likely over two hundred pounds or more each, and may take umbrage at mama's condition.

And one does appear where mama has broken brush, but looks only a second, then spins and is gone. The other, I presume, following.

"Get...get this load...," Alex is groaning, "...off

me."

She's five hundred pounds if an ounce. I hate to set my weapon down as the young ones may decide to even the score, but Alex is gasping for breath.

My rifle must be set aside.

Reaching over her I grab the far foreleg and sit back, then put both feet on Alex's side beneath the bear and heave for all I'm worth.

"Push," I yell at my squashed friend, and he does as I rock back and pull again, and he's able to slip out enough to breathe.

Then I realize Alex is covered with blood, it drips from his eye sockets and covers his throat.

"You hurt bad?" I ask what seems a stupid question

"I think…it's…bear blood," he manages.

Relieved, I take a deep breath and ready myself. Another heave for all we're worth and he's able to free a leg and push with it as well—and, with another mighty heave, he's free.

He stands, wipes his eyes, then, with hands on knees, gasping, looks at me. "You're bleeding, bad." With that, he pats himself all over face and neck and grins. "Chest hurts, but that's all."

I look down to see my shirt shredded at my side and four nice gashes where she's raked me with those three-inch claws. Thank God, only a half inch deep, but blood runs freely.

"We gotta stitch that up," Alex exclaims. "Then I'll butcher— "

"No...no sir. She had two young'uns, and they might yet slip up on us. We'll wrap this tight and shove off. If we gotta sew, make it later. Besides, I want a half-pint of Who Hit John first."

"You're right. Let's go. That was a damn fine shot. I hit her heart high but that wouldn't have stopped her. That brain shot was world class."

"World class lucky," I say.

"What is all the shooting?" Sarah says, taking a few steps our way the stopping short. "My goodness, that's a bear," she says. It's all I can do not to compliment her on her perception, but I quell my sarcasm.

"That is a bear," I manage. "Pack up. She's got family."

We hurriedly wrap my middle tight with a pair of cotton socks under a canvas strip that can be tied tightly, pack a little haphazardly, the shove off.

It's not more than a mile before the canyon narrows, makes a turn, and the rising sun is only a memory. The river is deeply shadowed and running hard, humping, and fast. If a rock takes us at the fifteen knots we must be travelling, even our thick hull would likely be broached.

Alex worries he has a broken rib or two. I'm soon to be sore-as-Hell, but at least have the bleeding stopped, and Sarah is still a debilitated mess.

What a time to take on a wild river and God only knows how many killer rocks, or worse, waterfalls!

Chapter Thirty-Two

———————————

As it happens, the cuts in my side are only a half-inch deep for an inch and a half or so, then for another three inches taper to a scratch. As much as I'd like an excuse to down a pint of whiskey, I decide against using a fishhook as needle and to keep the wound bound. It'll be badly scarred, but with a body covered with scar tissue it seems to matter little.

The good news is the river runs deep; the bad is the banks are more and more rock cliffs. And the river speed has picked up. As the river bends, there are spots where it's devoid of the morning light, then with a bend, suddenly well-lit. I'm happy to note the sky is not so gray and I occasionally catch a glimpse of some blue ahead.

Alex has named our craft Gertrude for some reason known only to him. I not only have no complaint but am amused by it. I only hope our little boat is not offended as we need her as friend for a long while.

We've gone no more than five miles when an ominous roar and rising mist ahead portends nothing good. I look for a place to shore Gertrude but set my jaw and ready myself as the walls lining the Salmon are nearly vertical.

"Hang on," I yell, "get to the bottom," I instruct Sarah, who moves slowly, as if she cares little about living.

Then our bow dips forty-five degrees as the river falls away, scoops a hog's-head barrel full of water from the frothing foam, then comes level. Thank God it was not a fall, only a very steep drop, and thank Him even more so there are no sharp-edged rocks awaiting us.

It has soaked Sarah, and I yell at Alex, "Dig a blanket out for her." And he does, but I don't let her off duty. "Sarah, use the pans and bail while Alex gets you a wrap."

"I'm cold," she replies.

"When we find a spot, we'll put in. Bail." And I'm pleased to note, she does. Alex is busy looking for obstacles, and I'm occupied with the tiller. Besides, moving will help keep her warm.

I watch her carefully, wondering if she's not considering throwing herself overboard and ending her suffering, but when she has the boat as dry as possible, wraps the blanket around her, bends and shivers.

It's a half hour before I'm able to ground Gertrude but do and we quickly build a fire and dry Sarah out, keeping her wrapped in the blanket while she sheds clothes and we hang them in front of the flames.

Alex pulls me aside. "Let's get her wrapped in tent cloth. Stopping will keep us in this damnable canyon until weather changes and we'll all meet our makers."

"Let's wrap her up and get back on the water."

We've begun our third day in the canyon, with Gertrude banging off a half dozen or more rocks and now seeping at the seams.

If that's the worst of it, you wouldn't be able to get the smile off my face.

Sarah is now eating—her appetite growing with every meal. And her eyes and color are returning to normal.

I have no idea how much longer we have on this damn water, that has been white twenty percent of the time and I'm surprised we're not all seasick, if seasick is the right term on a wild and wooly river.

And it's a good thing Sarah is functioning as she must constantly bail to stay ahead of our sinking. More than once we've have more than six inches of water in the bottom and it's not the wet or fear of sinking that's the worst effect of the flooding, it's the lack of steerage. As the craft grows heavier, she's less responsive to the tiller. Which means we're more likely to take a rock head on.

Were we not constantly worrying about dying a watery death the scenic trip would be invigorating.

More than once we've seen elk and deer populating the slopes, and mountain sheep have stood on the rocky cliffs no more than a stone's throw and stared as we bobbed past. Once we spotted white mountain goats high on a mountain cliff side. Bald eagles and Ospreys—fish eagles—have entertained us with their skill at scooping trout and what I imagine are salmon from the surface in the few slow spots and pools we've passed, and cliff swallows continually work the surface for insects.

Most of the hillsides are covered with pines, but larch are beginning to turn yellow, and cottonwoods that only occasionally dot the shoreline are turning yellow and gold.

It's late in the day when the ominous roaring ahead puts a chill in my backbone.

"Hang on," I yell, and watch carefully as Alex stares ahead, ready with hand signals. Then he signals a hard left and I comply. With the first deep dip we again scoop water, this time taking on at least a foot deep. Sarah is madly bailing, I'm trying to gain steerage with little effect, when Alex screams.

"Pray!"

Chapter Thirty-Three

But neither Sarah nor I take time to clasp hands together to entreat the Lord as we're too busy.

Gertrude dives straight down and, had we not been going so fast, both Sarah and I would have joined Alex in the bow, then we hit something ahead and are both thrown forward.

As the boat tries to right herself, Sarah plunges over the side, but Alex snatches the back of her coat and keeps her half-in-half-out of the craft.

Then we hit again and the bow shatters, somersaults, and we're all thrown out.

I hit the surface and fight to stay atop, but am sucked under into a roiling maelstrom. Tumbling, tumbling, then scraping a rock, then the bottom, I'm fighting to keep what breath I could suck in as I was flung overboard.

Getting my wits about me, I'm able to get feet under me and shove as I've never shoved before, for the light above must be the surface.

What seems an eternity, pulling with arms and

kicking, I break surface and gulp in air, getting some water in the process. Coughing and spitting, upchucking water, I'm finally able to concentrate on my circumstance.

Sarah! Alex! I think. And with panic in my voice, after catching a breath, yell for them.

I'm still bobbing in heaving water and foam, when suddenly I float into quiet water, and find myself entering a large backwater pool. I grab for a floating plank and realize it's Gertrude, destroyed, now in pieces.

But thanking a merciful God, I see both Alex and Sarah ahead of me, both clinging to shattered planks as am I.

As the water stills even more we paddle for shore.

We struggle out, and I fall face down. Solid earth has never felt so good, then I'm shocked to see Alex plunge back into the water and begin stroking hard.

Sitting up, I see his target. One of our lockers is afloat, only two inches of it showing above the surface, but showing. He reaches it and begins towing it ashore and yells to us. "Gather as many planks as you can, and look for the other locker."

I, too, hit the water and begin gathering planks, some only four-foot-long, most a dozen. I'm also able to find the mast, still wrapped in sail. Sarah works the shore, stepping into the circling water when a plank passes close enough.

When we've salvaged all possible, we collapse, and I can't help but begin to laugh.

"What's so damn funny?" Sarah asks, as Alex joins in with a guffaw.

I stop long enough to explain. "We're alive. Absolutely no reason to be. Talk about cheating fate."

Even Sarah smiles. "And I was just beginning to value the condition."

"Condition?" Alex asks.

"Yes. The condition of being alive."

All of us laugh.

Alex adds to the humor. "Should we say a few words over Gertrude's grave."

"Hell," I reply, "we hardly knew the old girl."

We laugh again.

"Ever build a raft?" Alex asks me.

"About to, I guess," I reply with a shrug. "But let's get a fire going, take inventory, and dry off first."

"A sound plan, my man. A sound plan. But a fire?"

As has always been my habit, I dig a steel and flint out of my pocket and display it, along with my folding knife. In short order, I'm peeling shavings and gathering kindling.

He grins. "By God, you're the one handy as a pocket in a shirt."

We manage to save both our handguns, one oar, coffee, some wet sugar and flour, a hindquarter and half the loin of the whitetail, two boxes of .44/.40

shells, a hatchet, some fishing gear, and the mast, sail, and halyard and twenty feet of additional three-eighths- inch hemp sheet line. The halyard and line are critical to our raft and the sail will serve as make-shift tent if we need shelter. Our cooking gear is long gone, other than one of the bailing pans that was tied to a single brass oarlock that was still attached to one of the gunnel planks. I've roasted many a venison steak skewered on a willow branch so we'll make do, and the pot will serve to cook greens and brew coffee which we'll pass around.

We could certainly be worse off. And we sure as Hell could be better off.

As it is we're all happy and slightly amused to be alive.

Before sundown we lay out our raft and it looks as if we'll end up with an eight by twelve-foot platform of lashed planks and deadfall limbs with the locker we've saved perched dead center. The tiller is lost but we can likely build a makeshift one.

It's coffee, a generous slab of loin, and the roasted roots of some cattails which grow in profusion on the edge of the slow water. We'd love to have saved some salt, but alas that's only a wish. Sarah does harvest a few handfuls of watercress and it's a nice garnish.

You'd think we were in a fancy Helena hotel about to have a cigar and snifter of brandy.

The supper meal seems manna from heaven, as miraculous as the bread of heaven that God provided for the Israelites.

And we sleep a well-earned one.

As shipbuilders we leave lots to be desired, but we're ready to launch before the sun is over the proverbial yardarm. She's a little low on the larboard side, but she floats.

I know Alex had a fair deal of gold coin aboard, and can't help but ask as we float out away from the shore, having to use our single oar as a sweep to get out into the current. "Did your stash of coin go to the bottom?"

"You gonna make me walk the plank if so," he asks, with a dubious smile.

"Nope, you gotta help us get to the Snake. Maybe then."

Sarah, getting some sass back, interrupts his response. "I'd guess Mr. Engstrom's financial condition is none of our concern."

"Well," I say with a laugh, "if you're not getting well enough to stick your nose into men's business."

"Men's business, humph!" she says, rolling her eyes.

"If it's any of either of your business," Alex offers with another wide grin, "I happen to have all my coin sewed into the back of this wide belt. So, we are still solvent."

I can't help but continue to tease a little. "And so, it's a sure thing we'll try and save you, should you go overboard."

"It's nice to be highly valued," he quips back.

We're soon tested by another set of rapids, but our work and the lines prove their worth.

By the time the sun nears the mountain tops to the west, we're on a wide slow section of river. Just as I decide it's time to make shore I spot a tendril of smoke and we press on until we see a squat dugout log cabin built into the slope up a hundred paces from the shoreline. Two large salmon are hanging from a drying line between cabin and a nearby ponderosa pine tree.

As we shore the raft, a barrel of a man, with a mane of hair to match a buffalo, a red flannel shirt, and elk-skin nearly-white pants tucked into calf-high elk-skin moccasins, walks from the cabin and stands with hands on hips. He yells something none of us understand. Then a slender comely woman in an ankle length buckskin dress, with a single crow-black braid of hair thick thick as her wrist hanging to her waist, walks from the cabin to stand beside him.

It seems we've reached civilization—as civilized as civilization is on the west slope of the Rocky Mountains.

Now, let's hope this big burly man is friendly.

Chapter Thirty-Four

We secure the raft and walk up the slope some twenty yards and stop, as the couple has not moved, merely stood with hands on hips.

"Wait here," I caution my companions, and move up another twenty paces then call out. "You folks speak English?"

"And French, Nez Pierce and some Latin," the big man says, then guffaws. He adds, "Tell the other gentleman and lady to come on up. We got a stew on, likely enough to share."

"And we have half a whitetail loin we can add."

"Bring it on. You got any whiskey?"

"Had some, but it's on the bottom of the Salmon along with most our goods."

"You come down the Salmon?" he asks, a little incredulously.

"We did."

"All the way?"

"All the way from the Salmon Trading Post."

"Well bless your souls. And it's fortunate you

still got your ghosts with your hides."

I move on up, and shake with the man, and note his ham-sized hands, then turn and wave the others up. Turning back to him, I decide on my new handle, and speak loudly enough that approaching Alex and Sarah can hear. "I'm Quincy McQueen, lately of Salt Lake City."

"You one of them Mormons?" he asks, eyeing me suspiciously.

"No, sir. Presbyterian, or was. Came out of Illinois before the late conflict. High country is my cathedral now." Again, I make sure my companions hear. "That's my brother Alex and my sister Sarahbell."

He smiles, showing a missing front tooth, and nods, seeming satisfied. "This be my woman, name of One Ear. Seems a bear or cougar or badger or some such gnawed the other off when she was a whelp. She don't remember what critter. I call her Pretty, which she seems to prefer. I'm Toliver Aloysius Tarver. Friends call me Bear."

I nod to the woman. "Nice to make your acquaintance, Pretty."

She nods, then walks past me and straight to Sarah, takes her hand and leads her to the cabin.

Bear has an old cap and ball muzzle loading rifle. As it's rut season for the elk, and I fancy myself a good caller, borrow his rifle, climb less than a mile with first light, call in a large bull, and I pay for our keep by dragging him down the mountain.

We spend three days healing and resting up. Sarah is better and better, and even her sense of humor has returned. She's bathed, and had her hair combed, and even asked Pretty if she had a curling iron.

And I caught her and Alex holding hands.

To my surprise, Bear has a small library, and I enjoy reading some classics, something I haven't taken time for in years.

The last day Alex and I spent rebuilding the raft, setting a mast slightly forward so we can make use of the sail for its stated purpose, or by using the boom as tent top using it to provide shelter.

Bear says it will snow soon, and as the wooly caterpillars have extra wool, it'll be a cold winter.

With his assurance it will be only two days of floating to reach the Snake and the post at Jawbone Flats, we set out. From Jawbone we can take a flatboat with a cabin all the way to the Columbia and down her to the Cascades, then a coach to below them where we can catch a sidewheeler all the way to Portland.

And we do.

Quincy McQueen, Sarah McQueen, and Alex Engstrom disembark a sidewheeler in Portland, U.S. State of Oregon, well rested, healed, and ready to start a new life.

To my surprise, upon wiring Miss Lizzy Perlmutter in Nemesis, I find she's relocated to San Francisco, where she owns a fine saloon named Lizzy's Lair.

She's not surprised to receive a wire from Quincy McQueen; returns a wire asking if I know a fellow by the name of Taggart McBain. My return wire says the last time I saw McBain was in a hotel room in Nemesis, Nevada.

Mr. Alex Engstrom has purchased a ship's chandlery and a vacant building next door, with the intent of adding dry goods and farm implements to the chandlery and a saloon. It seems his betrothed, a Miss Sarah McQueen, is interested in operating said saloon, leaving the bawdy house business and demon sap far in her past.

Knowing she's in very capable hands, even though Mr. Engstrom has offered me a partnership in the business, which I can pay for in time and out of my share of the profits, I elect to book a berth on the next steamship to San Francisco. He is kind enough to advance his future brother-in-law the necessary passage and, just in case, the cost of a return ticket.

I may return; then again, I may not.

A Look at: Mr. Pettigrew (The Nemesis Series Book III)

Nearly starved, missing half a leg, Beau Boone stumbles out of a cattle car into the hell on wheels Transcontinental Railroad town of Nemesis, and into gun smoke and battle to rival that of the war he's just escaped. Mr. Pettigrew and Miss Alice, of the Angel Cloud Saloon, befriend him, and soon he's sitting shotgun in the middle of a smaller, but equally deadly, conflict. And it's a war no one can win.

AVAILABLE NOW

ABOUT THE AUTHOR

L. J. Martin is the author of over three dozen works of both fiction and non-fiction from Bantam, Avon, Pinnacle and his own Wolfpack Publishing. He lives in, and loves, Montana with his wife, NYT bestselling romantic suspense author Kat Martin. He's been a horse wrangler, cook as both avocation and vocation, volunteer firefighter, real estate broker, general contractor, appraiser, disaster evaluator for FEMA, and traveled a good part of the world, some in his own ketch. A hunter, fisherman, photographer, cook, father and grandfather, he's been car and plane wrecked, visited a number of jusgados and a road camp, and survived cancer twice. He carries a bail-enforcement, bounty hunter, shield. He knows about what he writes about, and tries to write about what he knows.

www.ingramcontent.com/pod-product-compliance
Lightning Source LLC
Chambersburg PA
CBHW052044240626
47153CB00006B/2210